PHANTOM'S
healing

HURRICANE HEAT MC BOOK 2

I0594110

www.chellebliss.com

CHELLE BLISS

USA TODAY BESTSELLING AUTHOR

Publisher © Bliss Ink November 21st 2025
Edited by Silently Correcting Your Grammar
Proofread by Read By Rose & Shelley Charlton
Cover Design © Chelle Bliss
Cover Photo © FuriousFotog

ONE
POPPY

"IS IT ALWAYS LIKE THIS?" a snarky voice asks.

I almost drop my color bowl when I look into the mirror and meet the eyes of the client currently sitting in my chair. She's brand-new to the salon. She isn't supposed to be my problem, but she's been nothing *but* a problem since she walked through the door.

She had an appointment with my sister, but my sister is home sick in bed with the flu, along with most of the shop.

I knew when I opened my salon that owning a business requires blood, sweat, and tears. But nobody ever told me about all the illnesses that are involved—like fevers, coughs, and congestion.

Today is the last Saturday before school starts back after summer vacation. That means my salon—along with all the others in town—is packed with teachers needing haircuts and students wanting fun colors before they go back to the grind.

Busy Saturdays are one thing, but thanks to this nasty late-summer flu virus, I'm three stylists short and have clients backed up waiting in chairs.

I have been run ragged since I opened the doors, trying to cover as much of the work that I couldn't cancel and questioning every life choice that has brought me to this moment.

Another quick peek in the mirror confirms I don't look nearly as hot and flustered as I feel.

"No, it's not typically like this at all. Saturdays are always really busy, but usually, it's not quite so chaotic." My voice deserves an Academy Award for sounding professional and even perky. Though, inside, I feel like screaming. "This is absolutely not normal," I assure her. "I'm really sorry about the extra noise and wait time. We really try to make the salon experience luxurious, but…"

I start to smile, I really do, but when I meet her eyes in the mirror, this customer, Shayla, is scowling at me like she smells something foul. Her grumpy expression shakes what's left of my composure and calm.

I'm tired. God knows I've been tired for the last eight years. But in all the years I've owned this place, I've never had to deal with so many people out sick at the same time. I've needed to pee for the last forty-five minutes, and I'm so dehydrated, if I don't get a sip of water, I'm going to start coughing like my sister was when she called me this morning.

It's going to take every ounce of what's left of my charm to get through this day. While I know this can't be the greatest first experience for Shayla here, I'm doing my absolute best. I only wish that were enough.

"Half my staff caught the bug that's going around, so rather than cancel your appointment at the last minute, I wanted to cover you myself. I am sure next time you're here, things will be much quieter," I explain again, telling her the same thing I did in my voice mail messages—all of which she clearly ignored—from early this morning.

Shayla shifts in her seat so dramatically I have to yank my brush back so I don't get any color on a place I don't want it. Today is not the day for corrections. This woman doesn't seem like the patient type. I want to get her color done and move on, finish up her daughters, and just get through this day.

Shayla booked a color and cut for herself and her teenagers. This should be a large bill and a really nice bit of return business—if she ever decides to come back.

I wait until she stops fidgeting, then finish her color, peel off my gloves, and rally another big smile. "I'm going to go check Daisy's color. I'll be right back."

I'm already hustling over to another station, where I've got a bright panel of teal-blue color processing right around the younger girl's face, when I hear Shayla snap, "Can I get a magazine or something?"

"Oh yes, of course," I say, trying not to let my frustration show as I grab a few magazines from the table that is within arm's reach for her.

I smile at the adorable girl who's playing a game on her phone while I check her color. She has shocking blue eyes—crystal clear and bright like the ocean after a storm. She told me she's thirteen and about to start her last year of junior high.

"This is going to be beautiful," I tell her, getting sincerely excited. It's just one bold panel that frames her face, but it's going to set off her eyes beautifully. "You doing okay?" I ask her, folding the foils back down. "You need just a few more minutes."

This is what I love about my work. The technical aspects of making something artistic and creative come to life. Her hair was damaged by the at-home colors she used all summer, so I'm thrilled to see the blue saturation is turning out exactly the way I hoped.

"I'm good, thanks." Her smile is guarded but friendly, and she goes right back to her game.

Her elder sister is still in the waiting area, her head down, absorbed in her phone. I was hoping to get all three of them done close to the same time, but seeing how backed up we are, there is just no avoiding some waiting.

I head over to one of the voices who called my name earlier, my absolute favorite shampoo girl, Cynthia. She's giving me a look while she washes one of my regulars, an older lady who is so sweet and loving, I wish I could adopt her for myself.

"Everything okay?" I ask, immediately concerned.

My client Grace lifts a shaky hand toward me and clears her throat with a rattle.

"I know you're swamped today, honey, but do you think you could bring me some tea when you have a moment?"

Even though I have absolutely no time to run in the

back and make tea, Grace has been one of my most loyal customers. There were weeks in the early days when I first opened the shop that she was the only client I had.

She has a birthday party to go to tonight or else she wouldn't even be here on a Saturday instead of her usual Monday for her weekly wash and set.

I reach down and clasp Grace's hand in mine. It feels so frail and cold. "Are you feeling all right?" I bend low and ask the question near her ear.

She squeezes my hand and clears her throat. "My throat's just feeling parched today. You know me. I hate to be a bother, but…"

"You are never a bother. I'll heat some tea right up for you. Herbal? Something with no caffeine?"

"Perfect," she wheezes, the scratch in her throat almost making me cough.

Ugh.

I do a quick scan of the salon and see every single shampoo bowl occupied. The stylists are a blur of capes and brushes, curling irons and color carts. Every hand in the place is working frantically to manage their own clients. As much as I want to keep moving people through, there's no hand free to make tea now except mine.

Without wasting another second, I rush into the employee lounge and click on the electric kettle. It's ice-cold since I haven't offered tea to anyone since we opened, so it's going to take a couple seconds to heat up.

I wash my hands thoroughly since I just held

Grace's hand. It's going to take a miracle for me to avoid catching this bug, but I stopped believing in miracles years ago. I don't even let myself dream about them anymore. If I've learned anything in life, it's to keep my head down and rely on the power of my own hard work. I scrub viciously, willing those germs down the drain.

Just as the electric kettle chimes to let me know the water is ready, the lounge door opens.

"Poppy, the client at your station is asking if it's time to wash her out," my newest employee says with a frustrated frown. "I told her you set a timer, but she's insisting I ask."

"I'll handle it." I briefly close my eyes to gather my composure. "Will you take this tea to Grace, the nice older woman at the shampoo bowl? Make sure you give her a guest tray so she doesn't have to hold it while she's getting washed out. Put one of those honey sticks on the side in case she wants sweetener. I forgot to ask. Thank you." I hand the girl the mug of tea, but then I realize if I'm going to get through this day, I'm going to need more help.

"Sarah," I say, "I know you have no free hands, but can I borrow you, please?"

With the guests I have in the chairs and the colors and cuts I could not cancel, I'll be here tonight until way too late.

My son sleeps over at his best friend's house almost every Friday night so the boys can play together on Saturday while I work. I do the friend's mom's hair for free as a thank-you, because at times like this, when my sister is sick, Mom is off saving the city from itself, and I'm stuck at the salon, I don't know what I'd do with Jax if he didn't have someplace fun to be.

I give Sarah a list of things I need her to do, repeating them slowly and making sure she remembers to take Grace her tea. Then I rush through that long-overdue bathroom break. When I finally walk over to the new client, she's got her eyes closed and is frowning.

"Hi, Shayla." I try to sound upbeat as I peek under her foils. "Ready to wash?"

She draws in the world's longest sigh and lifts an eyebrow at me. "I've been ready," she says. Then she gets out of the chair and storms to the bowls like she owns the place, not me.

"Okay, great." My bubble of enthusiasm is bursting.

Just a few more hours, and I can go home and cry in private.

"Oh, I love this," I say, giving Shayla a hand mirror so she can see the back of her cut and color. "What do you think?"

She grimaces as she looks at her reflection. I'm holding the back of her hair between my fingers, lifting and fluffing it so she can see the layers and how the colors blend. "It's darker than I expected," she barks.

I feel defeated inside. The color is literally exactly what she asked for, and there's no denying that it looks beautiful. There's depth and subtlety to the dimensions of blond. She's going to be able to go maybe six full months without touching this, based on how slowly she said her hair grows.

She should love this result. I love it, and if I could see any flaws, I'd be the first to point them out and talk about redoing the work. That's how I've always done things.

"Darker, how?" I ask gently, twisting two of the big, shiny curls that I dried into her hair and arranging them so they are framing her face.

"You know what? Forget it. It's just hair. It's fine," she says, huffing and thrusting the hand mirror back at me. "Are my girls done?"

It's just hair. Hair that I've worked on for hours. Hair that she's going to wear on her head and look at for months.

Talk about insulting me, my time, and my chosen profession in one single breath.

But like she said, it's fine.

I'm fine.

I take the mirror and hang it back on the hook on the wall of my station. "Daisy is ready," I say calmly. "She's a doll." I point to where she's sitting in the waiting area. "Do you like the blue? I think she's really excited about it."

"I'm sure it's fine," Shayla says, snapping off her smock and tossing it over the chair. "I've got to make a call. I'm going to go out to my car for some quiet. It's so loud in here, I can't hear myself think. How soon until my girls are done?"

"Holly's washed, and I'm cutting her next. She

should be ready in about a half hour," I tell her, my stomach sinking.

The fact that she complained but doesn't want to talk about it and now wants to go out to her car... I can just imagine the crappy review she's about to post someplace. But that, too, is part of the burden of owning a business, so I lift my chin and give her a smile, sure that I'm pouring the last drops of my professionalism into my voice. That well is about to run totally dry. "Thanks so much for coming in today. I'll let you know as soon as the girls are ready."

I have no illusions that I'll be earning a nice tip or even a return customer after this, but I'm still going to give the elder daughter the beautiful cut she deserves.

Shayla storms into the waiting area and whispers something to her daughter, who looks up and gives her mom a look but then furiously goes back to her phone. When the woman is gone, it's like a storm cloud moves past the salon and the sun shines a little bit brighter.

Shayla's elder daughter is on her phone when I get to the station where Cynthia is putting the finishing touches on her blow-dry.

"Hi," I say brightly, and the girl's hands disappear underneath her smock. "Thanks for being so patient today." I turn to Cynthia. "I'll finish her up. Have you taken your break yet?"

Cynthia shakes her head. "I let the other girls go first since I'm the most experienced. I figured I'd stay on the floor in case you need me."

I'm so touched. I put a hand on Cynthia's shoulder and say softly, "Go on, hun. I've got it from here."

"Okay, but if you need me," Cynthia says quietly, "I'll come right out."

I want to hug the girl, but the more time we spend talking, the more behind I'll get. I give her what might be the most genuine smile of the day and turn to the teenager waiting in the chair.

I finish blowing out her beautiful long hair, so dark it's nearly black. She must get it from her father because her mother's natural shade under the complex color I just did is an ashy blond.

Thankfully, I'm almost finished with the drying because the girl seems agitated. She keeps looking down at her phone, moving her arms under the smock and hiding what she's texting. This doesn't seem like normal teenager stuff. She flicks her eyes to mine in the mirror, looks worried, and goes back to pounding away at her phone.

Whatever is going on is none of my business, so I put away the hair dryer and grab my shears from a drawer. "So, Holly, we're just freshening up your long layers? You want me to leave as much of the length as I can, or did you come up with any other ideas while you waited?"

When I turn back to Holly, her younger sister Daisy is standing at my station, glaring. "Tell her," Daisy says to her sister, her voice practically a growl.

Holly looks at me, and a fiery red blush pops across her cheeks.

"Hey." I rest my hand on Holly's smock-covered shoulder. "What is it? Is there something wrong with your hair?"

I don't know who to be more worried about right now. Daisy, who keeps throwing nervous looks back at the door, or Holly, who is fidgeting in the chair like she's ready to run.

Daisy shoots me a look. "We're so sorry. Holly, tell her."

Daisy runs back to the waiting area and sits, but she stares daggers at us from across the salon.

I lower my face a little so my mouth is close to Holly's ear. My mom instincts are not just tingling. There's a three-alarm worry fire in my belly. Two kids furiously texting, an angry mom, and now, something they are afraid to say. If these girls are in some kind of trouble—or, God, maybe their mom is—no amount of work stress is going to stop me from doing everything in my power to help.

"Honey, what's wrong?" I keep my voice low so the whole salon hopefully can't hear me. "What does your sister want you to tell me?"

Holly's lips tremble like she's about to burst into tears. "Would you maybe let me use your phone? Your cell phone."

My phone is tucked into the back pocket of my jeans, but before I hand it over to a nearly crying teenager whom I don't know, I need her to tell me what the heck is going on.

"My cell phone is right here, but why can't you use yours? What's happening?" I press.

The hum of the hair dryer clicking on at another station muffles her voice, but I can make out enough of what she says for her words to hit me like a flamethrower to that ember of worry in my gut.

"I'm so sorry," she whispers miserably. "My mom is gone. She left. She texted us to call a rideshare when we're done and to pretend we're coming outside to get her. She wants us to leave without paying the bill."

TWO

PHANTOM

"CAMERAS ARE FOR SHOW." Our point man for this deal, a guy I know only by the name Elliott, discreetly angles his chin toward the security equipment mounted above us. "System's not connected."

I shake the man's hand and search his eyes. "Right. We checked that out before we agreed to meet here."

He doesn't need to know how much intel we've done on this operation. He just needs to know that we have. This ain't our first rodeo, but it is our first moving this amount of product for this particular client. We don't normally meet, but for a job this big, I demanded an in-person location on a busy Saturday when the recycling center would be open with lots of foot traffic.

I'm supervising this gig. Viper, our enforcer, and Hawk, our road captain, are handling it with me while Savage is parked in a strategic position in case anything goes down.

None of us are wearing our club leathers or

anything that could make us easy to identify later. Viper and Hawk look like they're dressed up for Halloween in soccer dad outfits. They won't exactly blend, but with their golf shirts, sunglasses, and baseball caps, they'd be tough to pick out of a lineup. That's all that matters.

Despite the summer heat, I'm in a long-sleeved button-down shirt that covers my tattoos, black jeans, and dark glasses that I only remove when I look Elliott in the eye. Elliott and I nod at each other, the CEOs of our respective organizations, so to speak. Then our guys get to work.

Savage and I walk back to our bikes and climb on, but we don't leave. We watch, taking everything in.

This job means a shitload of cash for the club. And when a job pays that good, there's always a reason. My guys are on high alert for any sign of cops, feds, or even the competition. We're not the only ones in town who want to be on the receiving end of a paycheck that's going to be this big.

Even still, not one of us wants anything to go down that could land us in lockup. Or, in my case, back in.

It was one thing going away when my daughters were little. They didn't understand why Mommy and Daddy didn't live together or why sometimes Daddy had to go away for months—even years—at a time. It was normal for them, and they just lived it, spending Father's Day visiting me across a table with more supervision and cameras than a reality TV set.

But they're teenagers now. They know what it means if Daddy gets arrested. Convicted. *Sentenced.*

I don't give a fuck what happens to me. Sometimes in this life, the juice is worth the risk of the squeeze.

But the older my girls get, the more I realize that nothing is more important than being here for them. And I don't just mean alive—I mean not behind bars and being free.

I've got a bigger plan in mind, and while this deal is probably the worst possible way to go about it, the money we make is money I need if I want to get my girls for good this time.

Taking care of Shayla, though, has proven a longer and harder job than taking her out would have been. But I'm not that man. I don't hurt women or children—not unless they come for me and mine and ignore a clear first warning.

I give nobody second chances.

One of the reasons I'm here today at all is so I can take care of Shayla and my girls the legal way. The right way. And there's no chance I'm letting that plan go to shit. No matter what.

A sudden buzzing breaks through my focus on the handoff taking place in front of me. When I'm on a job, no one gets through to me on my cell phone.

Nobody except my daughters.

I don't bother to check the first buzz of a text alert. I've got a special tone set up so I always know, day or night, if Holly or Daisy is trying to reach me.

But the first buzz is followed by a second. And then the damned phone starts ringing.

I swipe the lock screen and almost dismiss the messages until I catch a look at the text. I glare down into my phone, trying to make sense of what I'm reading.

"You got business?" Savage lifts his chin at me. "Take it. I think we're cool here."

I nod at Savage, my eyes never leaving the quiet transaction happening ahead. When they look about done, I scan the text from the unknown number.

Dad, it's Holly. I'm borrowing a phone because I don't want Mom to know I messaged you. Daisy and I are in trouble. You've gotta come now.

Like a volcano bubbling before it bursts, my guts are churning before the blood turns to ice in my veins. Whatever the fuck is happening, I need to get to my daughters, and I need to get to them *now*.

I listen to the voice mail, which is incredibly hard to hear because Holly is whispering from some place that's noisy as fuck. She leaves an address and says to get there as soon as we can, or to call this number when I see the message.

"You got this?" I shoot Savage a look.

He nods slowly toward Hawk and Viper, who are discreetly putting bags of aluminum cans inside the covered bed of a pickup truck instead of dropping them here. A couple of those bags will have cans filled with a product my guys have been hired to move. The rest are just normal, nothing to see here, empty cans gathered up for recycling. The only difference is we're taking them out of the recycling facility when we leave.

"Looks like they're about done." Savage nods.

I make eye contact with Elliott, who's playing point

on this deal, so I make my presence and authority known. I may be leaving, but I'm far from uninvolved.

Then I fire up my bike. "Any problems, you handle it any way you want." I glare at Savage, and he grins.

"Wouldn't have it any other way."

I know he'll handle this shit. He's been by my side, at my back, or even in front of me, taking heat since he patched in to this club.

Savage is ex-military and has the most time in legit life out of everyone in the entire club. He is the one I trust to run into trouble first and not to look for a way to save his own ass. He's got more than just the drive and the loyalty. He's got training, guts, and passion.

"I'm out," I say before peeling out. If my kids are in trouble, no amount of money or danger will keep me from getting to them.

I head for the address my daughter sent, trying my best to keep myself from blowing every light and running every stop sign. Holly gave me no clue what kind of trouble they are in, but this isn't the first time my kids have used someone else's phone to reach me.

To say the situation with my ex-wife is complicated would be putting it mildly. The power could be cut at the house. She might have left the kids alone with no dinner while she's off with her latest fuckboy. Or there could be something more twisted that my brain couldn't even dream up. Shayla wasn't always the person she is now. Fuck, maybe she always was and I just didn't see it...didn't want to.

All I know is, the sooner I get my girls away from her, the better.

I race into the small parking lot at the address Holly sent me and drive toward the only building with lights still on. It's not even dinnertime, but it's Saturday, so most of the businesses are dark. I head for the glass door and yank with such force I'm surprised I don't pull the thing off its hinges.

I storm into the place and immediately see my girls. My vision goes red, and I blindly run toward them.

"Come here." I open my arms, and they both jump up and run toward me. They tackle me in a bear hug, and I close them in tight, relieved as fuck that no matter what trouble they are in, they are alive. They don't look hurt. They're okay.

As soon as the hug ends, the adrenaline kicks in. The girls both start talking over each other, but I'm scanning the premises for threats.

"Dad, we're so sorry—"

"Dad, Mom wanted us to—"

I hold up my hand and take in the scene. The first thing I see is a woman. A stunningly beautiful woman whose intense stare makes every inch of me take notice. She's got long, dark-brown hair curled and styled to perfection. But she doesn't look stiff or made-up. Her full lips are glossy, and she wears sparkly makeup around her big brown eyes.

I look around, but I don't see Shayla and, even more bizarre, the place looks calm. Holly and Daisy go back to sitting on a plush tan love seat covered in cream pillows. The woman is sitting in an armchair that looks fancier than anything I've ever owned. Her legs are crossed, and she's sipping tea.

I can tell from all the sinks and shampoo bowls that I'm in some kind of beauty shop, but there are so many plants and seats, this place looks more like a café or somebody's home. It's nice and all, but my blood pressure won't chill the fuck out until I know why I'm here.

"You said you were in trouble," I say, turning toward my girls. "What happened? Where is your mother?"

Holly and Daisy trade anxious looks. My elder daughter is a lot more forgiving of her mom, and she just looks down at her hands. Daisy stands up and rushes back into my arms, her eyes filling with tears.

"Dad." Her words come spilling out so fast, her mouth pressed against my chest, that I almost can't understand her. "Mom brought us to this new salon for back-to-school styles and said we could get whatever we wanted. So, I got color, which is extra, because I've been doing the color myself at home—"

"Hold up." I reach for Daisy's shoulders and lean her back to study her face. There's no fucking way my kids would send an SOS because of a goddamn haircut. "You said you were in trouble."

"I think I can explain." The woman who's been noshing on lunch with my kids stands up and extends her hand. "I'm Poppy. This is my salon."

I look down at her hand skeptically, not sure if she's part of the problem or trying to help. I give her hand a quick shake, but I don't give her my name. She gives me an apologetic smile, and I notice tired-looking purple shadows under her eyes.

"Your wife—" she starts.

"*Ex*-wife," I correct.

She licks her lips and nods. "Ex-wife. Well, Shayla is new to the salon. She came in for services today with your girls and left without paying. I tried charging the card we put on file when she booked the appointment, but it was declined. I don't have any way of charging her for the services she got for herself and the girls today."

I must look confused because Holly stands up. "Dad, Mom left us here after her hair was done." She holds out her phone to me, and I read the group text she sent to both girls.

We're not paying that bill, so I want you to get the hell outta there and take an Uber home when you're done. I'll meet you there. Be chill about it. I don't need her calling the cops on us like that last place.

I nearly crush Holly's phone in my shaking hands, but I know how expensive the damn thing was. I bought it for her three months ago for her fifteenth birthday.

"Your mother tried to bail on the bill?" I look from Holly to Daisy. "She pulled that shit before?"

That's when the floodgates open. Daisy is in full meltdown. "Dad, yes, but it wasn't our fault. We didn't know. The owner of the last place called the cops on us and said if we didn't stay until Mom came back and paid, she'd press charges against all of us, including

Holly and me. This wasn't our idea, Dad. We swear we didn't know."

Holly is deathly quiet, and when I look at her, she's too pale. "Dad, I tried to make sure she wasn't planning anything like that again. I asked her if she had the money this morning. But you know what she's like." Holly looks down at her feet and laces her fingers together so tightly, a knot even tighter forms in my gut.

Daisy points to the salon lady, still talking through tears. "Poppy has been so nice to us, Dad. She didn't threaten to call the cops. She didn't yell. She even bought us food because we've been here all day, and we were starving."

My kids, whom I pay everything for—child support and then some—were *starving* and had been dragged into some bullshit haircut scam?

"How much is the bill?" I ask, keeping my voice as calm as I can until I have all the facts.

"Let me get the total." Poppy gets up from her seat and walks to the back of the salon, where I see a counter and a mounted tablet that doubles as a mini cash register.

Goddamn it.

This is the worst time to notice, but this woman is fucking gorgeous, and Shayla is proof that I don't have the best track record of finding the good ones.

As I watch her walk across the salon like she's strutting on a private runway, I can't stop my mind from imagining those long legs wrapped around my neck, all that hair sweaty and tossed across my pillows.

I tug on my beard and try to ignore the way my

fingers itch to cup her full ass. She's tall, stacked, thick, and... *Fuck*.

I turn away from scoping out this woman and lower my voice to talk to the kids. "You're really all right? Other than being hungry and your mom running out on the bill, you're safe?"

Now that I'm with my girls and I know I'm going to fix whatever's got them in a panic, my blood pressure is dropping.

It's damn hard not to stare at Poppy's perfect ass in dark black jeans and the long waves of hair that almost reach her waist, but if there was ever a perfect distraction from a beautiful woman, it's my kids.

Holly nods and Daisy sniffles. "Dad, you don't know how bad she's gotten. Mom left us here and didn't care what happened. What if Poppy had called the cops? That last lady wanted to have us arrested, Dad. We're just kids. What would have happened to us?"

At my daughter's fear and pain, my vision goes dark with rage again. I've been locked up. Arrested. Searched and booked. Abused and neglected. There is nothing, and I mean nothing, on this green earth that I wouldn't do to protect my kids so they never know that kind of shame and powerlessness. I'm strong mentally and even more so physically, and God knows I've made a lot of bad choices—still do. Part of playing the game is paying the price, and I've paid dearly.

But this... Shayla setting up my daughters like this... Not once, but twice.

"When did this happen before?" I bark. I need to

know. Not because it matters right now, but it matters in the long run to my plan. "Forget it. You can tell me later. Did your ma pay that other place?"

"She did, but that was the worst part," Holly says, her cheeks still looking too pale. "She had the money, Dad. She was just... I don't know. Trying to get away with something."

The dull echo of Poppy's heels on the floor pulls my attention back to her. My body ricochets from rage to lust as she offers me a device, her soft hand touching mine as she hands the tablet over. I grit my teeth and will myself not to act like a horny teenager, and I look down at the itemized bill. The total has so many zeros in it, I about shit myself.

"This is for haircuts?" I sputter. I'm not excusing Shayla's shit, but maybe she was the one getting scammed.

Poppy nods, the long curls of her hair bouncing. "Shayla had a full-head highlight, cut, and style. That service can start at three hundred for a senior stylist, and there is a slightly higher charge for long hair." She looks me over like she's trying to figure out if I'm going to fight her. "Then the girls..."

I do the math in my head, and I guess it all adds up. I've been getting haircuts for as long as I can remember from the bitches who hang out at the compound.

After prison, anybody with a gentle touch and a willingness to do the job was my only qualification. It must cost a pretty penny to keep these plants alive and lush couches looking so clean.

"Dad, these are totally normal prices. The other

place was even more." Holly's at my elbow now. "And we really should tip."

Tip? Sweet baby Jesus, no wonder the women at the club are all too happy to drink our free beer and eat our food. They must be broke on haircuts. I know what I've been paying for the girls' essentials, but this shit?

I drew the line this past summer on fake nails because that's a money pit I'm not ready to fall into for kids too young to hold down their own jobs. I'm going to have to work a lot more gigs like the one we had today if my plan to have them full time is going to work.

I blow out a long breath and hand the tablet back to Poppy. Her face shadows like she expects me to bail on the bill, but I reach into my back pocket and peel off a wad of hundreds—enough to cover the bill and food.

"Here." I am about to hand her the money when I turn to Holly. "How much do I tip?"

She grins and stands beside me, lacing her too-thin arm around my waist. "Dad, she took really good care of us before all this. The food, letting us call you. At least what you'd tip in a restaurant. If you pay on the tablet, you can pick a percentage if that's easier."

It's not easier. I don't leave a digital trail until I absolutely have to. I peel off two more hundreds and hold them out to Poppy.

"No, really, it's okay. You don't have to do that," she says, holding her hands up in front of her. "I'm grateful you were willing to take care of the bill. It's not just the materials, it's the time."

I shake my head, not needing to hear the details, and

hold out the cash until she takes it. "You took care of my girls when their own damn mother couldn't be trusted to." I pull out my phone. "Is this your number? You let them use your personal phone?"

She nods.

"You keep my number in your phone. You see my girls on the schedule again, you call me." I sigh. "I'll cover it. No questions asked."

I turn to the kids. "What are we going to tell your mother?"

Holly's face drains of the little color that's left, and Daisy puts her hands on her hips.

"I don't want to go home to her right now. I mean, she literally drove off like no one would dare to arrest two kids alone. What if they did?" Her brave anger starts to crumple, though, and she looks like she's going to cry again. "Don't make us go, Dad," she whimpers. "Can we stay with you tonight, please?"

I open my arms, and both girls slam against my chest. I kiss the tops of their heads and notice for the first time how beautiful their hair looks. I stroke a big blue curl that falls along the side of Daisy's face.

"You got that here?" I ask her.

She beams up at me and nods. "So much better than the at-home dye Mom lets me use."

I look past my daughters' heads and catch Poppy staring at us.

"You did good work. If anything could make my girls more beautiful, it's this." I kiss the kids again. "This is what we're going to do. I'm going to message your mom that you told me you were getting your hair done, so I stopped by to see it. I won't say anything about the bill. I'll just tell her you asked to come crash with me for the night."

I don't say that this will, no doubt, start World War whatever we're up to now. Every communication with Shayla is like an act of aggression, but there's no way I'm sending the kids back to her tonight. She drew first blood by abandoning them in the middle of a fucking scam. I pull out my phone and shoot off a text to the bitch.

"Girls, thank Poppy for taking good care of you. I rode up here on my bike, so Shadow's going to come meet us with a pickup."

The kids start to gather up their dirty plates and cups, but Poppy shoos them away. "It's okay," she tells them. "I have to clean the salon anyway."

"Go on and wait out front," I tell them. "Make sure Shadow can see you. I'm going to talk to Poppy for a minute."

The kids thank her, and I notice Holly leans in like she wants to hug Poppy, and Poppy nods, then holds the girl close.

"We're really so sorry about this," Holly says again, her voice tight. "I hope you know it was never our idea."

Poppy puts her hands on Holly's shoulders and lowers her head to meet Holly's eyes. "You did the right thing telling your dad," she says warmly. "And I know you didn't mean to hurt me. Adult things like this are complicated, but it's okay. Now, I want you to put this behind you and feel confident with your new hair.

Okay? If you want to come back, you are always welcome in this salon."

Fuck. Her words hit me like a boot to the gut. She's smart. I'm so goddamn happy she said that about the hair. The last thing I need is for the kids to feel guilty every time they look in the mirror, walking around with a visible fucking reminder of what their mom is. What she tried to do to them. *Dammit all to hell, Shayla.* Fuck that bitch and the bullshit she puts on these truly good girls.

Holly and Daisy head out front, their pep almost returned to normal levels. Once we're alone, I turn to Poppy.

"I didn't say thank you," I tell her in a low voice. "This is a debt I can't repay, you being here for my girls." I search her face. "But I've got to ask. With a bill that big, why didn't you call the cops?"

Now that we're alone, I look my fill. Poppy isn't just attractive and well put together. Sensuality oozes off her in waves, and I don't know if it's just that I haven't shot a load in a while or if it's her full tits, generous ass, and long hair, but I'm again imagining all the things I'd like to do with this woman in a place far more private than this waiting area.

She meets my eyes, her big, doe eyes matching my intensity. "As soon as your girls got the text from their mom, I could tell they were not involved. They were shocked and so upset. All they kept saying was their dad was the best and he would take care of everything," she says simply. "I'm a mom. There's nothing I wouldn't do to protect my son. I wanted to give you a chance to make it right, and you did."

"And if I hadn't?" I ask, flicking an eye to her hand, and notice no ring but a small tattoo etched on her ring finger. "Would you have called the cops or sent your husband after me?"

At my words, her gaze drops. "I, uh, don't have a husband. I'm a single mom. And I don't know what I would have done. I'm just grateful you made this easy. So, I should be thanking you."

That's not something I'm used to hearing. I'm used to people thinking I'm a fuckup. That I always choose the hard way, always go too fast, too deep, too everything.

"It says a lot about you," I tell her. "Beautiful, smart, and caring."

She blushes at my compliments, and the pink staining her cheeks only makes her that much hotter.

"I'm sorry about all this. Shayla wasn't always such a bitch," I tell her, shaking my head. "Maybe it's partly my fault. God knows I wasn't always the easiest man to be married to. I'm kind of a handful."

A smirk covers my face almost despite myself. I don't tell her that the work I do is far from legal. I just don't profit off the backs of innocent people. The men I deal with know exactly what game we're playing.

"I believe you are a handful." Poppy's words are breathy, with a hint of something more. The electric current in her voice travels through my body like I've stuck my finger in a socket.

We fall silent, the tension in the room thick and

sensual as smoke. Then Holly knocks on the glass door, breaking the moment.

We both look up and see a pickup idling.

"That's my ride," I tell her, turning to leave. "Remember what I said. I'll cover their bill. No questions asked."

I don't know how soon they'll need to come back, but it won't be soon enough. Seeing this woman be so sweet to my girls moves something in me, something I've kept locked down hard deep inside. I turn away from it, from her, and head toward the door.

"You didn't tell me your name," she calls after me. "Or should I just put 'Holly and Daisy's dad' in my contacts?"

I stop at the door and look her over from head to toe, then back at her stunning face. "Phantom," I tell her. "You can call me Phantom." I'm about to leave when I turn back. "I'll be seeing you, Poppy."

She looks flustered, and I give her a grin before heading out to the lot, slapping Shadow on the shoulder, and handing him the keys to my bike. Then I get into the truck with my kids.

As we pull away, I look through the glass window of the salon. I see Poppy at the door, just watching. Before the warmth pooling in my gut makes me do something stupid, I look over my shoulder, back up the truck, and pull away.

THREE
POPPY

I DON'T KNOW how long I stared out the front doors after that pickup truck pulled away. Maybe I'm dehydrated or just plain exhausted—God, I hope it's not this flu—but my body is doing funny things. I keep thinking about the man who just came into my shop. All Holly and Daisy could talk about was how their dad would make it right, how he would take care of everything.

I wasn't so sure.

But the girls seemed so sincere, so genuinely horrified by what their mother tried to do. What kind of person would I be if I didn't give them the benefit of the doubt?

And then he did come through. Rode in here like the hero of the story and made everything right for his girls. But I have to say that man was nothing like the hero I expected.

Phantom is attractive. There's no way around that. His jet-black hair and piercing blue eyes are otherworldly. And the way he smiles behind his thick beard makes my heart beat funny.

I'm not used to men having this effect on me. After losing Michael, I locked up my sex drive and threw the key so deep into the ocean, it would take a search and rescue team to find it.

But something about Phantom is different. Maybe it's not just the muscles I could see through his jeans or the hint of tattoos I could make out on the tops of his hands.

After years of being in Mom mode, I know it takes more than some gorgeous eyes to make me remember I'm still a woman. The more I think about him, I realize that what makes him so undeniably attractive is that Phantom is a *dad*. Not just a part-time, pay-the-bills, phoning-it-in dad, but he's involved and hands on.

He didn't just call in with a credit card. He showed up. He noticed the kids' hair. He literally came to his girls' rescue.

God, how I wish my son had a father like that in his life. Jax used to have that. Not that he remembers. He lost his dad when he was just a toddler. The biggest crisis Michael solved for our son was picking up dropped toys and cleaning up spilled juice. The routine stuff of daily life that now, like my husband himself, is only very, very vague memories.

I would never, ever put my child in a situation like what Shayla did today. Still, I can tell you that if Jax ever got into trouble, I know that Michael would have been every bit the hero my son deserves. No wonder a guy like Phantom has pushed all the right buttons—even the ones I didn't know I had.

I feel like a traitor even thinking that, and I shove any dark thoughts about Michael away.

But as I stand with my face pressed to the glass like a puppy that's been left behind, I can't deny that Holly and Daisy's dad didn't just save the day for his kids. He made everything right for me too.

Without even knowing that I needed a hero, he came in and saved me from what would have been a terrible financial loss. I mean, the salon wouldn't have closed because I couldn't collect on three haircuts and color. But it's not like I can afford to do all that work for free.

How long has it been since I've had anyone in my life who took care of something like that? Whether it's a blocked toilet, a late bill, a hungry kid, a skinned knee —I've been a one-woman show for eight long and tiring years.

I try to convince myself that what I'm feeling isn't attraction, that it's relief. And it's better that I focus on that—the money he saved me, the headache of having to decide whether to call the police. He took care of a messy situation. That's all this was. Fluttery feelings in my belly mean absolutely nothing in the real world.

And just like always, the moment I have to myself ends far too soon. A buzz from my phone snaps me back to the present. Salon that needs cleaning. Stylists out sick. There's so much work to do, it's time to lock my libido back up and return to reality.

I pull my phone from my back pocket. When I see

the name on the caller ID, my heart immediately plummets into my belly.

"Tera?" I don't even say hello. Tera is babysitting my son. After all these years watching Jax on Saturdays, Tera would only call me at work if there was a problem. The question comes tumbling out of my mouth before I can stop it. "Is everything okay?"

"Poppy, I'm so glad I caught you. I know you've got to be swamped, but Jax spiked a fever. I think he's caught this bug that's going around. I gave him some cold juice, but he's just been lying on the couch for the last hour looking miserable."

"Oh my God, Tera. I'm so sorry and so glad you called."

Tera and I chat for a minute about the boys' sleepover, and I promise to get there as soon as I can. The second we hang up, I run back to the lounge.

"Cynthia," I blurt out.

She whirls on her stacked black heels.

"I'm sorry," I say, trying to calm my voice.

"What is it, Poppy?" Cynthia almost drops the boxes of supplies she was organizing. "You need me?"

I explain the situation and ask her if she can lock up the salon. "Just throw the food that's up front in the trash, but leave everything else for me. I'll handle it tomorrow."

I regret the words as soon as I say them. Normally on Sundays, I bring Jax into the salon with me. While he gets one morning of unlimited screen time to play video games and watch YouTube videos, I clean the salon from top to bottom. Water the plants. Rearrange and stock the stations. It's a day we spend together, but it doesn't feel like work. I love this place, and usually, Jax is more than happy to come along and even help—as long as I add a little extra to his allowance for the chores.

If he's sick, I'm going to have to hire someone to come in and clean. On short notice, that's not going to be cheap. Even worse, if he must miss the first week of school, I am going to have to hire a sitter or stay home with him. I'm doubly grateful to Phantom now. I'm going to need every penny—including the tip—that he left me.

I grab a bottle of shampoo, conditioner, and a heat treatment spray for Tera as a thank you for watching my sick kid. I just hope Jax doesn't spread this through her whole house.

Once I get to Tera's, I feel even more devastated. Jax is so weak and sweaty, he can hardly walk himself out of the house. He's a tall kid, like Michael was, and so skinny for his age. He's had to mature faster, being an only child with only one parent, but at times like this when he's sick, it's not hard to remember that he may be ten, but he's still a little boy.

"Baby." I hold him close once we're safely back inside our house. I feel his forehead, which doesn't feel too hot, and I hope the fever's broken. "I'm going to get the thermometer and some meds to help the fever. I'll make you any dinner you want. What are you craving?"

Jax rubs his eyes and peers up at me, looking far younger than his ten years right now. It breaks my heart. "Soup?" he says miserably. "I know it takes a long time to make, but..."

"Soup," I assure him. "Go climb in bed and put on a movie. I'll be up to check your temp as soon as I change."

Our house is small but cozy. Jax has an attic bedroom with a bathroom upstairs, while I have the primary bedroom with an en suite bath down on the first floor. Michael used to have the attic as an office. When Jax was a baby, he slept in a bassinet in our room and later a toddler bed.

We were in the process of looking for our next home, someplace bigger we could grow into. But we were struggling to afford more house when life—or, I should say, death—derailed all our plans.

So now Jax uses his father's office for a bedroom, and I have a room on a totally separate floor where I can cry myself to sleep at night without my son overhearing. Thankfully, I cry a lot less than I used to. Not never, but less.

My feet are throbbing from standing all day. Just because my body is used to working long days doesn't mean I don't feel broken down by the end of a long week. But I change into my yummiest sweats and a slouchy, loose T-shirt and move into Mom mode.

I bring Jax a thermometer and take his temp.

"It's 103," I tell him. "No wonder you feel like shit."

I use the word I don't allow him to say just to get a reaction out of him.

"Mom," he chuckles. "Don't you mean crap?"

"You tell me," I tease, sitting on the edge of his bed and ruffling his hair. "Do you feel like crap or like shit?"

"The second one," he groans, closing his eyes. "Do you think you could hand me my headphones? I want to listen to a movie, but I don't think I can keep my eyes open. The light really hurts my head."

"Don't be surprised if listening hurts your head too. It should get better once the medicine kicks in." I get up, grab the headphones from his desk, and slide them over his ears. "I'll be back with soup," I promise. "Rest if you can, baby."

I turn off his lights and close his bedroom door, then pad down the stairs.

I dig in the freezer for some chicken and start a pot of water to boil. I'm going to use store-bought chicken broth, but the chicken and veggies will be hand-cut by Mama. Just like my baby likes it.

I stand over the sink rinsing the carrots and stare into the pretty twilight. The sky above our small backyard is pristine and clear—a gorgeous blue. I find my mind drifting back to the blue eyes of the man in my salon.

Phantom.

What an odd name. It must mean something, but I didn't have the energy to think about it at the time. He was massive—far taller and more muscular than his long-sleeved shirt revealed. Now that I'm home and alone, without the noise and chaos of the salon, thinking about his thick thighs in those dark jeans... I'd actually have to be dead not to notice how attractive he was. I mean, there's no denying where his daughters got their stunning blue eyes.

I spin away from the sink and grab a cutting board. I've got to work out some of this energy. Is it horniness? My God, it's been so long since I've been with another person. I don't think I'd even remember how.

After losing Michael, I went completely empty. As a newly single mom of a toddler who could hardly make it an hour without crying, I mummified my heart, wrapped it up tight just to survive the pain. Of course, I locked down my body too.

But something about Phantom has me intrigued. I shake my head, a small smile on my face. He's obviously not a regular salon client himself. He doesn't look like the type to pamper himself. I imagine he either cuts his own hair or has a girlfriend do it, because of course a man who looks like that has a girlfriend. He must.

A wave of guilt and sadness washes over me. It's not as if I think Michael would expect me to stay single forever.

As I chop the veggies for Jax's soup, I try not to think about how amazing it would be to have a partner. Someone who could rub my back, help with the chores, or even just talk to me while we make our sick son soup. No matter how long Michael has been gone, the longing for a partner to share this with—the good and the bad—never goes away.

There's no instruction manual for how to live your life after that life falls apart. Divorce is hard—God knows so many of my friends have lived through the trauma of a relationship ending—but I'm the only woman I know who was a widow with a two-year-old in her twenties.

I'm confused why I keep picturing Phantom's thick black hair, the beard that covered a wide, strong jaw, and his dazzling blue eyes. I'm lonely, sure, but before I can scold myself for thinking like a hormonal teenager, my phone rings. My heart catches for a minute, and I wonder if it's *him* calling me.

Oh my God. I must stop this.

I answer the phone just for something else to think about, and thankfully, it's my sister. I put the call on speaker while I finish making soup. We catch up about her symptoms, and I make myself a cup of tea. I tell her about her new client and how she almost stiffed us for three services.

She sounds as drained as I feel. "Good God, Pop," she groans. "I can't even with people sometimes. I'm sorry I wasn't there to deal with it, or maybe it's better that I wasn't."

My sister is nothing if not honest. It could have been an ugly situation if Clara had been there. I love my baby sister, but I thank my lucky stars it was me who ended up dealing with Shayla today.

"It was fine," I assure her. "The girls' dad came and took care of it. Problem solved." I don't tell her about how attractive Phantom was, though. For some reason, I want to keep that detail to myself. "Do you have what you need? I'm making Jax soup if you want a delivery?"

"With noodles?" She makes a yum sound into the

phone. "If I didn't know how shitty your day was, I'd beg you to bring me some. I'm good. Just tired and sore from coughing. But if you make extra and have the energy tomorrow, I won't say no to a care package."

"Deal. Love you, sis. Drink lots of fluids."

We say goodnight, and I mentally calculate all the things I need to do. Thinking about the growing list makes me so exhausted, I sit down for a second and rest my head in my hands, and I sip my tea to steady myself.

I'll get through this just like I have every other thing over the last eight years.

At least, that's what I keep telling myself.

FOUR
PHANTOM

"SO, what do you girls drink? Juice?" Stella is behind the bar, sounding confused and looking nervous. She bites her lip and motions behind her. "We have milk back in the kitchen."

I head back behind the bar and pour myself a cup of coffee because I can't start my day without it. "They're teenagers, Stel, not aliens." I lift a brow at her, and she shrugs but doesn't look any less terrified.

Letting the kids have a sleepover at the compound on a Saturday night threw a wrench in the usual drinking, drugging, and fucking that takes place here. But one look from me silenced anybody who might have had any complaints.

After catching up with Savage about the rest of the job, I spent the entire night in my room, watching movies and eating pizza and popcorn, listening to my girls laugh, gossip, and complain.

I've never been happier.

God, I love my kids. Other than a few tense calls to

my lawyer, the night couldn't have gone better. And thanks to a very successful deal, I've got the funds to make sure, this time, everything goes to plan.

"I don't know for sure, but I heard from Sarah that Tyler and Kiernan are both in my homeroom." Holly's voice is low as she looks down at her phone. The girls are sitting on barstools pulled close together, so Daisy barely has to lean over to peer at Holly's phone.

"Tyler's in your homeroom?" Daisy asks. "Isn't he a senior?"

"I love boy talk." Stella leans forward on the bar with a grin. "Do you have a picture? Are you friends? Or is Tyler something more?"

Holly shoots a look at Stella, then very obviously nods her chin toward me. I hold my coffee in one shaking fist and point a finger first at Stella and then at Holly.

"No boys. Ever. Not until you're twenty-one. Make that thirty-one."

"Dad!" Holly rolls her eyes. "I'm talking *about* him. Not to him. I don't even think he knows I exist."

"Oh, he knows." My nostrils flare as I practice my anti-boyfriend snarl.

Daisy shakes her head. "Dad, you'd like him. He has a job. He works at the mall, and he's, like, really nice."

"You're still in junior high." I raise a brow so high I can practically feel it hit my scalp. "How the hell do you know a high school senior, Daisy?"

Stella's eyes go wide. "I think that's my cue to excuse myself."

"Daisy." I poke my finger even harder against the

top of the bar. "Answer me. How do you know this boy?"

She rolls her eyes even more dramatically than her sister did. "I don't know him, Dad. He's Holly's friend. All I know is what Holly told me. And what she's shown me."

"*Shown you*?" I practically squeal the words. I don't think I've hit an octave that high since I took a billy club to the nuts during a fight my first run inside. "Give me your phone." I hold out my hand. "You're grounded for eternity." I turn to Stella. "What do you know about homeschooling?"

Both girls are laughing, and Holly clutches her phone to her chest like I'm joking.

I'm one hundred percent fucking serious.

The last time I went to prison, I was away for over a year. If you don't think you miss out on a lot in a year with kids, let me be the one to tell you you're wrong.

A year is a fucking eternity when it comes to little ones.

While I was away, Holly developed some minor food allergies. Daisy went through a phase where she refused to take baths. They had nightmares, growth spurts, friends, and talents. And I missed it all.

I worked hard to make up for lost time—not that it felt like work. These girls are the only thing I've done right in my life. That and building this club.

I have brothers who would kill and die for me, and I'd do the same for them. I have a home and plans. Money in the bank and more stability than an asshole like me ever thought possible.

Ever since that last stint inside, I haven't gone more than a couple of days without seeing the girls, without knowing their friends, their schedules, what they like to eat, and what they listen to.

The only thing I don't know anything about is this pissant *Tyler*.

Before I lay into the kids about the nunnery as an alternative to public school, Savage approaches the bar, his expression deadly serious.

"We got a problem," he says cryptically.

I have a feeling I know what the problem is.

"Keep it contained. I'll be right there."

Holly and Daisy don't seem to be paying attention, but Stella is.

She puts a hand on my arm. "Do they like pancakes?" she asks.

I nod. "Girls, I'm starving. You feel like going into the kitchen and making pancakes with Stella? I'm in the mood for chocolate chips."

Daisy is off her stool in two seconds. "Yes," she squeals, her excitement so adorable, I almost forget the Tyler problem.

There's an even bigger problem outside, and this is one I *will* protect my kids from.

"Holly." I nod at my eldest. "Go on into the kitchen for a bit. You can even have a cup of coffee if you want it, but just one cup." I'm bribing her, but I could give a shit if she goes on in.

She nibbles on her lower lip like she's aware of what's about to go down, but she doesn't argue. She climbs off her stool and starts to follow Daisy and

Stella into the kitchen, but then she stops and turns back.

"I love you, Dad," she says quietly, throwing herself into my arms. "I'm glad you brought us here. We'll be okay if we have to go."

Rage and relief pour through me like hot lava. I hold Holly tightly and rest my chin on top of her head. She smells expensive, like fancy-salon shampoo.

For a moment, I see the image of the hot salon owner in my head, but I drive it away and hold my daughter close. "I love you too. Now, go block this Tyler kid's number in your phone. I'll be back in a sec."

Holly giggles but throws a worried look back at me.

"Go on," I assure her, my heart bursting and breaking all over again.

She knows what's about to go down. She's probably been on the receiving end of a thousand shitty texts from her mom since she woke up. I know I have, and I've ignored every single one.

This moment was always going to come eventually. I've never been fool enough to think Shayla would make anything easy.

"She's raising hell on the front drive," Savage says in a tight voice. "Threatening to bash in your brains. Typical Shayla stuff."

I draw in a shaking breath and clench my hands into fists. "She got a weapon? Who's out there with her?"

"Shadow and Viper." Savage chuckles. "Her only weapon is her big-ass mouth."

"You need me to do something?"

I turn to the voice behind me, ready to take out my

rage on whoever thinks it's a good idea to interrupt me. One of our prospects, Dylan—also known as Jizz, thanks to a stupid mistake he made while giving a piss sample at the doctor's once—is hovering close.

"Back the fuck up," I tell him. "You'll know if I want you anywhere near me." Stupid fucking prospects, desperate to prove their worth and pissing me off eight ways to Sunday. I instantly feel shitty because he's only trying to help, and I'm really only pissed at Shayla.

I turn to shove open the front door and immediately hear the hollering and cursing that my ex is famous for. "Make sure the cameras are rolling," I tell him as I step outside.

"You motherfucking ugly-ass nobodies!"

Shayla may have had an expensive haircut and color yesterday, but she looks like straight-up trash right now. Her face is red and sweating, and she's wearing dirty clothes. Her too-tight tank top is stained, and her cutoff shorts expose way more of her body than I ever need to see again. She probably was out partying all night and came right here from whatever club let her in.

Shadow has his hands in the air, and he's clearly trying to reason with her. It would be funny seeing her slip around the gravel in flip-flops with heels on them if I weren't damn sure she'd sue the club if she fell.

Viper's got his arms crossed over his chest, looking like he's having a hell of a time keeping a lid on his temper. Viper doesn't have kids, doesn't have an old lady, and doesn't have two shits to spare.

His nickname is apt because he's probably the most lethal of all of us—one hit from that guy would knock

Shayla into her next lifetime. Viper knows I need the cameras recording this shitshow, or I have no doubt he'd have already shown her ass the way back to her car or the inside of a coffin.

"Shayla," I say, choking back what I really want to say. "What's your problem? This is private property, and you know you're not welcome here."

She surges at me, rushing across the gravel drive to shove me backward with both hands. "You're my fucking problem, you filthy son of a bitch. Where are my kids?"

The blood literally boils inside my veins. For a minute, the world goes dark, and I see red. I have never laid a hand on Shayla, but at times like this, the desire to choke the fucking air from her lungs is so strong, I have to jam my hands into my pockets to stop my fingers from betraying my self-control.

"Shayla, you need to calm the fuck down." My voice is steady, but I know I'm pushing her buttons.

"Fuck you!" She explodes forward, shoving me again, and I have to take a step back to regain my footing. "And fuck you!" She goes wild, turning on Viper—a man she knows will not hesitate to put her ass in place. And yet, like a Florida hurricane touching down, she can't stop herself, whirling, her expensive hair flying, as she grabs the front of his shirt and yanks. "I know my fucking kids are in there. I'm going to call the cops if you don't send them out right now."

Viper makes a move to restrain her, but I tear a hand from my pocket and hold it up to stop him.

I don't even need to bait this woman into her worst behavior. She's doing fine all on her own.

"The kids aren't coming out, Shayla," I say calmly.

I'm thanking my divorce lawyer in my head right now. Shayla and I filed when I got convicted the first time, but we still loved each other back then. Our custody agreement was mutual and flexible, so I'm not violating any law by keeping the kids with me. I can have them any time I want them, no restrictions.

"The hell they aren't!" She makes a big show of pulling out her phone and punching in 9-1-1. "Let's see what the cops have to say about that."

"If you call them, I'll press charges. I've got a lot of shit you don't want dragged out in front of a judge." I point to the bubble mounted over the compound door. "A lot, Shayla." A lot more than her acting like a fool on my driveway, thank God.

"For fucking what? Trying to get back my kidnapped kids?" She starts to lose steam, because she knows damn well she's on the losing end of this fight. All I have to do is push a little harder, and I know she'll snap and probably commit enough criminal acts to ensure the cops would have plenty to charge her with.

I stand perfectly still, not baiting her. Just waiting until she chills the fuck out.

She's a monster, so she does what I expect. She bursts into sobs. "I want to see my babies," she cries, not a single real tear rolling down her cheeks. "Why didn't they come home last night?"

Viper shifts uncomfortably in his boots, and Shadow rakes a hand roughly through his hair. I hate to air my shit in front of my brothers, but I need witnesses for this, and they know it.

I don't want to take away Shayla's right to see her kids, but the last few months, she's become unstable. It's one thing to hate me and to show up here causing a scene. But there've been other things.

Too many other things.

At the beginning of the summer, she left the kids home alone. When she didn't get home by eleven, the kids' weekend bedtime, they started calling and texting her. Nothing. Not a word in response. The girls had the good sense to call me at three in the morning. When she didn't respond to my texts offering to come pick her up, bail her out, whatever she needed, I went and got the girls. We reported her missing at noon the next day.

She eventually stumbled home and tried to blame me for forgetting that she had plans for a few days with a new boyfriend, but that was not only a lie, it was the last straw. With a little help from a private investigator, I found out what that little disappearing act was about.

And it's time Shayla knows everything that I've been doing since then.

"Look," I tell her, trying real damn hard to see the woman I once loved in the mess of a human in front of me now. I fail miserably. I don't even recognize her, but it still hurts me to tell her this. "Shayla, my attorney filed an emergency petition with the court. I'm going to get full custody of the girls. They're not coming back with you, so I need you to get yourself together and go home."

I've never seen a woman stop crying so fast.

"Like hell you are," she says, her voice low and mean. Gone is the hysterical Shayla. This version of her is far scarier.

That's why I have no choice. I must take these kids from their mother.

"Shayla, you fucking listen, and you listen to me good," I say, meeting her lethal tone. "You think I don't have ways of knowing you got yourself locked up in June? Fucking shoplifting like a goddamn shithead at the mall. What the fuck is wrong with you?"

She starts sputtering, but I hold up a hand and tell her to keep her goddamn mouth shut.

"If you don't listen, I'm going to let Viper do whatever it is he's been wanting to do since you set your sloppy ass on compound property."

"Fuck you, Viper. You lay a hand on me, and you'll lose that hand so fast..."

"It's over, Shayla. Whatever you're going through, get some help. But you're not dragging the kids through the shit with you."

"You son of a bitch," she seethes. "After all the years I supported your sorry, loser, criminal ass." She lunges at me then, clawing at my face, but I'm faster, stronger. I grip her by the forearms and stop her before I lose an eye.

"You already know that theft of goods or services over $750 is a felony in the state of Florida because of that little stunt you pulled back in June." My tone is a low warning. She stops fighting me and listens. "And what you tried to pull at the hair place yesterday? I know because I fucking paid it so that salon lady wouldn't call the cops on your children. Your *children*, two minors, who you tried to involve in your commission of a crime—and not your first. You know what could have happened to you or to them?"

I release her arms roughly and take a step back. "You're lucky I took the kids before the goddamn state did."

I turn my back on her and head back toward the door. "Don't set foot on this property or any place else where the kids are, or where I am, or I'll add a restraining order to the filing."

She's standing there with her hands clenched into fists, listening and looking shocked, as if the full gravity of what's happening is finally hitting her.

"Don't contact me or the kids directly again until the court sorts shit out. You got my lawyer's number. You got something to say, say it to him. Get yourself together, Shayla. For your own sake, if not for the girls'."

"If that isn't the fucking pot calling the kettle black. You're the goddamn criminal, Phantom, you know that! The girls don't respect you. I don't respect you." She hauls off and spits, and I feel the dampness of her spittle strike the back of my arm.

I turn so fast I kick up a cloud of gravel dust. "I loved you once," I spit out, waving my hand from her sloppy expression to her filthy clothes. "And I don't know who the fuck this mess is anymore. Get the fuck out of my life." Then I turn to Viper. "Make sure she gets safely to her car."

He and Shadow take that as their cue, and they

surround Shayla, not touching her, but letting her know without saying a word or lifting a finger that her visit here is over.

When I go back inside, Savage is right on my ass. "I'll send a copy of the video to your lawyer," he says.

I nod but don't say more.

A part of me feels sick to my stomach. Bile and something sad, darker floods my mouth. I never wanted this for my kids.

But people change.

I know that better than anyone because I'm not the man I used to be. In some ways, I'm way better. In other ways, far, far worse. But at least I can take care of Holly and Daisy. I just hope they're going to be okay with that.

I take a few breaths, run a sweating hand through my beard, and swallow back the sour taste in my mouth while my heart rate slowly comes down. The kids are sitting at barstools, laughing loudly and eating pancakes. One of our prospects is chatting up Stella, who points to me as I approach.

"Your plate is in the oven staying warm," she says. "Want me to grab it?"

I nod and grumble my thanks.

Daisy is leaning over Holly's arm, making the kind of giggling sound that can only mean they are talking about a boy. My stomach rolls over in my gut. The kids aren't kids anymore. They are young women, and if this Tyler thing is really something I need to worry about…
Fuck.

I've been a single dad forever. But a full-time dad to two teenagers is something else entirely.

When Stella brings the warm plate and sets it on the bar counter, Daisy points to a pancake that looks like an oval smear with wheels. "I tried to make you a motorcycle, but it didn't exactly turn out."

I look down at the plate, and a sudden lightness floods my chest. Making pancake animals was something I used to do when the kids were small. They all looked like shit and nothing like real animals, but I'd make the girls guess what they were. I'd act offended and shocked by their very reasonable guesses, and when I'd finally tell them some random, impossible animal, they would laugh and squeal.

These girls may be young women, but they are still those kids. My kids.

I pick up the motorcycle with my bare hands and pop the whole thing into my mouth. "Best pancake I ever tasted," I say, talking with my mouth full intentionally. "It looked exactly like my ride."

"Dad." Daisy covers her eyes. "Your teeth are full of chocolate. Gross."

I wash down the pancake with coffee when the phone in my pocket rings. I'm prepared for it to be Shayla, but the caller ID says it's my lawyer. I set down my coffee and turn away from the bar. "Hey," I answer.

"I got the tape," he says, without so much as a hello. That's what I love about the guy. We're cut from the same cloth. No bullshit. "This is going to be helpful. I filed an emergency petition, and I expect a hearing to be put on the calendar. But I want you to get a statement from the salon owner, the one from yesterday. You think you can get that? And save the evidence from the girls' phones. I'll need screenshots of the texts from Shayla telling them to run out on their bill."

"Consider it done."

"I'll call you next week when I know more." And just like that, the call ends.

I head back to the bar for the moment of truth. I don't want the kids to know all the details. They don't need to worry about the legal shit. For now, what matters is that they're okay, and I just hope they're okay with what I'm about to tell them.

I climb onto a barstool next to Daisy. "You know your mom's not in the best place," I say. "I've asked my lawyer if we can file some paperwork so you two can come home with me for a while. We'll work out getting your stuff, and you'll be able to see Mom after the lawyers handle their shit. But how would you feel about staying with me? Not here. My house."

Daisy immediately climbs off her stool and throws her arms around my neck. "I want to redecorate my room."

Holly nudges her in the back and frowns. "Dad, I want to stay with you, I do, but is Mom going to be okay? You know how she is."

Daisy drops down onto her own stool again and pulls a face at her sister. "It's not our job to worry about her, Hols. Do you think she was worried about us yesterday when she just left us?"

Holly shrugs. "I don't know what to think."

"Daisy's right," I say. "It's not your job to worry

about your mom. It's time for her to take care of just herself for a while." I reach past Daisy and tap Holly on the nose. "And you too."

She smiles a little at that. "We can still go to the same schools and everything?"

I glare at her, my lips pulling into a frown. "If this is about that Tyler kid…"

"Dad." Holly shakes her head. "Stop. Nobody wants to change schools in their sophomore year."

I assure her that everything will stay the same. The only change is they'll get to decorate brand-new bedrooms at my place.

Holly looks troubled, but she hugs me hard. "Can we go now?" she asks.

"Go get your stuff from my room. I'm going to finish these motorcycle pancakes."

The girls run off to my room to pack up the few things they had with them when I picked them up from the salon. I've got a house not far from the compound with plenty of rooms that will need to be decorated now that they are going to be used full time.

I take out my phone as I eat. The pancakes are damn tasty. Warmth floods my body as I pull up the unknown number that is still in my phone. I change the contact to "Poppy Salon Lady" and realize I'm smiling.

My girls love me; I know they do. And they want to come stay with me, which is enough to melt my chrome and steel heart. But thinking about Poppy makes me feel something altogether different. I'm looking forward to something. Looking forward to moving my girls in. Looking forward to texting the hair lady with the eyes and ass that I can't stop thinking about.

"You look happy." Stella clears away the girls' dirty plates and gives me a smile.

I grunt and focus on my phone. Business me and Dad me don't mix often, and I don't need anyone at the club knowing too much about my personal life. What they've seen already is enough for a lifetime.

I open the text messages, but suddenly asking a stranger to submit a statement to the court over text doesn't feel right. I decide to pay the walking fantasy a visit and ask in person.

The corner of my mouth picks up in a half smile.

Happiness.

It's something I only feel around my kids, but there's no denying I'm smiling just thinking about the sexy salon owner.

Maybe Stella isn't wrong.

FIVE

POPPY

TURNS OUT, my chicken soup does not have healing powers. Jax was down for the count and missed the first three days of school. Thankfully, the salon is closed Sundays and Mondays. Clara recovered enough to go back to work and cover for me while I stayed home, but that meant more juggling in my schedule. By Thursday, when Jax is finally back in school and I can get back to the salon, it feels like Saturday all over again.

Canceled and rescheduled clients, a packed day, nonstop calls. By ten in the morning, I wish I had five sets of hands.

I'm at my station consulting with a regular client about a cut when I hear the rumble of a motorcycle. I can't believe my stomach does this fluttering thing at the sound. That man has ruined me. Every motorcycle I have heard for the past four days has my body responding like I'm one of Pavlov's dogs.

I try my best to ignore the growl of the engine outside and focus on my job.

"So, do you think I can pull off a pixie?" My client—who has never taken chances with her hair before—is pulling up pictures on her phone to show me when the salon door chimes.

I flick a glance toward the door, and then those butterflies in my belly take flight like a flock of seagulls competing for a snack.

It is him.

Phantom is here.

But this time, he looks a lot different.

Scarier and, somehow, even sexier.

He walks up to the front counter, his motorcycle boots thudding heavily against the floor. He's got dark glasses over his eyes, which he pulls up onto his head, and instead of the long-sleeved shirt, he's wearing a leather vest and a tight gray T-shirt that reveals arms covered in tattoos.

"Poppy?" My client swipes to close the app with haircut photos on her phone.

Without realizing what I'm doing, I look past my client to check my hair and makeup in the mirror.

"Yes, yeah, let's do the pixie," I say in a rush, trying to channel my excitement into something that matters.

When I look up and see the confusion on my client's face, I immediately feel like a fool.

"Is everything okay?" she says in a low voice, like I'm about to let her in on a secret. Her eyes lock on Phantom. "That looks like trouble."

"Trouble?" I'm confused. "Why do you say that?"

One look across the salon has me realizing that the client in my chair isn't the only one who's noticed

Phantom's presence. A number of my customers and even my stylists are looking him over, a nervous tension simmering under the quiet coffeehouse playlist we've got on.

"He looks like he's with that biker club, the criminal one," my client says quietly. "They have a bad reputation, Poppy. They're supposed to be into some shady shit. Is the shop in some kind of trouble?"

I can't even process what she's saying.

The man who swooped in and saved his children, who paid their bill, no questions asked, is a criminal? I mean, he rolled off a wad of hundreds, but lots of people still pay in cash. My client Grace doesn't even have a debit card and pays in twenty-dollar bills every week when she comes in for her wash and set.

"No," I say, trying to reassure myself as much as my client. "There's no trouble here. God, no. I do his daughters' hair."

"Oh." My client relaxes slightly and reopens her app.

"Let me just go see if he needs something. I'll be right back." I wave to Cynthia to get the client shampooed, then I head over to the front counter.

The way I'm drawn to Phantom's dark beard, full jaw, and piercing eyes has me feeling things, really feeling things that I haven't felt since Michael and I were young, and I'm not sure I like it.

I approach the counter and tap him lightly on the arm. His bare skin is hot, light hairs tickling my skin, and I immediately pull away. "Hey, can I help you with something?"

I don't know what I expect of a man who looks like he does, but the smile he gives me is so big and genuine, his eyes seem to turn from midnight blue to navy.

"Hey there, gorgeous. Good to see you again," he says, scanning the shop full of women, many of whom are looking right back at him. "Looks busy as hell in here. Any chance I can get five minutes in your office or something?"

My stomach sinks. I can't imagine what he's here for and could possibly need to talk to me about privately. Maybe he wants his money back... I think back over what my client said. If he's really with some kind of criminal club, maybe he's...

I'm spiraling. I don't know what he's here for, and there is no need to expect trouble just because he's a biker.

"Five minutes," he says. "I promise."

His smile melts me inside, and I immediately stop doomscrolling possibilities in my brain. I did nothing wrong. He hasn't done anything wrong.

In fact, if anything, he stopped something bad from happening here. Whether he is connected to criminals or is one himself, I'm going to give the guy five minutes of my time and then show him the door.

"I have a client getting shampooed." I nod. "I have a few minutes. I don't have an office, but we have an employee lounge. Follow me."

I head toward the back and feel the searing gaze of my sister as we walk past her station. Phantom follows me too closely for me to say anything he won't overhear, so I don't say anything. I just focus on not tripping over my heels and getting past the heavy stares of my customers and staff.

"Mary," I say, noticing one of the shampoo girls putting away product in the storage closet at the back of the lounge. "Can we have a minute, please?"

She turns and sees Phantom, and her eyes go wide. "Yeah, of course," she says, hastily replacing boxes of color, then scurries out onto the floor.

I motion for Phantom to take a seat on a leather love seat covered in plush faux-velvet pillows, then I drop down into an armchair, my knees feeling wobbly.

Phantom turns to look at the love seat like he's afraid he's going to break it, but then he carefully lowers himself onto it.

"I'm sorry for dropping in like this," he says, his voice going tight. "Won't be a regular thing. I have a favor to ask, and it didn't seem like the kind of thing to say over text."

A favor? This man wants a favor from me? All sorts of scenarios flood my brain, but I rush to the most obvious one: he wants his money back. I can't imagine what else he could want. But after all the extra expenses the last couple days, I really can't afford to give away my time and services. I don't have enough time as it is. Was his paying the bill just an act to look like the hero in front of his kids? My anxiety and anger must show on my face because he suddenly looks incredibly serious.

"Look," he says, leaning forward. "I wouldn't ask if

it weren't for my kids. I know you said you're a single mom, so I thought I'd shoot my shot."

I swallow hard and brace for it. "What do you want?"

He draws in a breath. "What happened here the other day, with Shayla trying to run out. It's not the first time she's pulled something like this, and without getting into the weeds, there's been other shit." He rubs his brow, and I notice the detailed and intricate tattoos on his right arm. Some of it looks rough and faded, but his left arm is full of colorful, newer tattoos and a crazy amount of muscles.

"What can I do?" I ask, doing my best to focus on his eyes, not his beautiful arms.

"I was hoping you'd write up a statement about what happened so I can give it to the court. I don't want to put you in the middle of anything, but I'm filing for full custody of my kids. My daughters are happy about it—thank God they want to stay with me—but Shayla, not so much. Having something from you about what happened here could help the judge make a decision." He shrugs. "But if it's something you're not down for, I understand. No harm done if you'd rather not get involved."

My heart rate slows a bit as I process what he's asking me for. It's not money. He actually wants my help?

"Is that all I'd have to do?" I ask. "Just write a letter?"

Just then, the door to the lounge swings open, and my sister sashays toward the sink. "Oh, hey. Am I interrupting? Don't mind me. I'll just be a minute." She stares at Phantom so hard, I'm afraid she's going to lose her eyelash extensions.

I draw in an annoyed breath and wave toward Clara. "This is my sister," I explain. "She's just about—"

"I'm Clara." She's suddenly right up in his face, her hand extended. "And you are?"

He looks from me to her, the severity of our conversation gone from his face. "Phantom," he says, standing to shake her hand.

Oh God. That was the absolute worst thing he could have said.

"Phantom?" Clara lifts a brow then fans herself with the hand he shook. "Sexy and mysterious?" She turns to me. "Whatever this is, I love it for you."

"Oh, for God's sake, Clara." I shake my head. "This is the man who covered his daughters' bill the other day."

Recognition lights up her face, and she turns her attention back to Phantom. "My sister didn't tell me you were gorgeous and that you were coming back."

"Clara." My voice does nothing but bring a smile to Phantom's face and fuel my sister up even more. We should have left the salon to talk. I should have known my sister would butt all the way into something absolutely not her business.

"What?" She puts her hands on her hips and looks at me. "Is he not single?" She turns back to Phantom. "No disrespect, but come on, look at him." She motions toward him. "Although, don't take this the wrong way, but who does your hair? You—"

My meddling flirt of a little sister literally takes a step toward him, her fingers wiggling like she's about to run them through his hair, when I stop her. "Clara. He's here because he needs me to write a statement about what happened. Can you not touch the man's hair and just give us a minute, please?"

She does the exact opposite. She plops onto the love seat next to him and nods sympathetically. "That's heavy," she says, still eyeing his hair. I'm not convinced she's not going to start trimming him right now. "What do you need the statement for? The cops?"

I cover my face in my hands, not sure if I should apologize to Phantom or tackle my sister.

"For the judge," Phantom says, looking both confused and a little amused. My freight train of a sister has that effect on people. "I'm trying to get full custody of my daughters."

Clara nods vigorously, as though she's actively a part of this conversation, which, now, she is. "We're really busy today, but of course she'll do it. When do you need it by? Do you need it emailed someplace or printed? What's your email?"

Phantom looks at me, and I shake my head helplessly.

"She's like this," I tell him. "Let's ignore her." But then I grimace and hold back a chuckle. "So, do you need it emailed? When do you need it? And I guess I should ask if there's anything specific you need it to say?"

Clara crosses her arms as if to say she was asking all

the right questions before I butted into my own conversation, but I refuse to look at her.

"I'll text you my lawyer's number," he says. "Send it all to him. That way, it goes right to the court from him, and no one can say I messed with it."

I nod. "I'll do it tonight. While it's still fresh in my mind."

He stands to leave, but then he stops and meets my eyes. "I can't tell you what this means to me." His voice is deadly serious, and I know what a big deal it is for him. If I had an ex and the roles were reversed, I'd have shown up on Phantom's front door Sunday morning after the whole thing happened, begging for him to document it too.

He flicks a quick glance at my sister and then meets my eye. "I want to do something to thank you," he says. "Can I take you to dinner?"

"Yes." Clara stands up and points at me. "Yes, you can take her to dinner."

"Clara, no. Jax just got over a flu bug, I don't have a babysitter, and…"

"I'll babysit." She cocks a brow at me. "Or you can ask Mom. One of us will watch Jax."

"He's not asking me on a date, Clara, for God's sake…" I look at Phantom. "I'm sorry. My sister is—"

He doesn't let me finish. "Bring your boy," he says. "I don't exactly have childcare myself, and I can't send the girls back to their mom's yet. I'll bring them too."

"A family date," Clara says. "Even better. She says yes."

"Okay, out. Go." I point to the door. "Don't you have clients processing?"

"Shit." Clara frowns. "Okay, I got to run. Bye, Phantom. So nice meeting you."

She flounces out of the lounge, and my shoulders sag in embarrassment. "I'm sorry about my little sister. She's always been that way," I tell him. "She's hard to ignore, but I've had years of practice. It gets easier."

"She's got good ideas," he says, his voice a sensual purr. "A family date sounds about right."

My breath catches in my throat when he says date.

"I, uh…" My mind is spinning, whirling. "You don't have to do that. I'm happy to write the letter for you."

"I want to, Poppy. I'd like to see you again, ideally some place other than your work. I'd like to do something nice for you."

I want to doubt that he's really asking me out. I want to think this doesn't mean anything.

The man's eyes are locked on mine. He's intense, but in the best ways. I feel a flush creep its way along my chest, and I have to look away.

He's too attractive. His strong jaw covered in thick black hair, the concentration that lines his brow as he looks me over. I shiver, every nerve ending in my body awake under his gaze.

I can't go on a date with him.

But it's not really a date if we bring our kids, right? Maybe it's just a friendly little thank-you dinner. I could do that, right? He's just being generous so he doesn't feel bad about asking me to write the letter.

I'll agree, and I probably won't hear from him again.

No matter how much I tell myself I shouldn't want to hear from him again, I feel instantly disappointed at the idea.

I'm out of my mind.

I've been locked down with Jax and his flu for too long. I need to tell this guy yes and send him on his way.

"Yes, to dinner." I nod. "You have my number. Send me your lawyer's contact information, and then, uh, I guess we'll be in touch."

"We will." He nods, then pulls the sunglasses over his eyes. He turns to leave the lounge, but when he reaches the door, he turns back. "Thank you, Poppy."

I can't see his eyes, but the growl in his voice sends every tiny hair on my arms to attention. I plaster on a smile and wait until he's left the lounge to sink back into the chair. Sweet Lord, that man. The letter. His kids. My kid. A date?

He's got me so tongue-tied, I'm even thinking in single syllables.

Phantom. The gorgeous man who literally is going to haunt my dreams. It's just dinner. Just a letter. What could possibly go wrong?

Yeah…I know.

This has trouble written all over it.

SIX
PHANTOM

I WAKE up early Saturday morning to another raging hard-on. The dream I had about Poppy ended with me doing filthy things with that full mouth of hers. I've had the same dream every night since she agreed to have dinner with me.

If things were different, I'd pick a woman at the compound and work out this frustration the right way. But I'm a full-time dad now, and that means the only release I'm getting is with the woman in my dreams.

I take care of business thinking about Poppy's big brown eyes, then climb out of bed, the faint light of early morning starting to make it past my room-darkening curtains.

The house I live in now is nothing like the places I grew up. I shove aside the curtains, and instead of a graffiti-covered alley with overflowing dumpsters, junkies, and sex workers, I see nothing but blue and green.

My large, open backyard runs right up to a small

dock I built with my own hands. I have a couple of kayaks and some inflatable tubes that the girls have floated on every night until the bug spray failed them and they came running in for dinner.

I crack my window and let in some fresh air. It's peaceful. No concrete jail yard. No drunken prospects puking on the gravel.

The sound of water running through the pipes reminds me that I'm not alone. Two teenagers bring more noise, and God, the smells—all good, mind you, but the body sprays, hand lotions, and shower gels that seem to stink up every room make me feel like I've been dipped in fruit-flavored candy.

And I love every single second of it.

I head down to the garage for a workout, lifting weights and running on the treadmill beside my bike until I'm wrecked. When I go back inside to shower, Daisy is in the kitchen, sitting at the table in her pajamas with a glass of juice and her tablet.

"You're up early," I say, heading to the cabinet. "It's Saturday. You can sleep in, you know."

"Dad, how old did you say Poppy's son was?" she asks.

I shrug. "Don't remember." I load up the coffeemaker and throw her a look. "Younger than you, I think. Why?"

She waves her hand. "I want to start babysitting next summer. Maybe Poppy's son can be my first client."

I wipe my sweaty forehead with the hem of my T-shirt. "Sounds like a plan," I tell her.

"What kind of restaurant is it?" she asks. "Where are we going?"

The blue stripe of color in her hair is tangled at the top of a messy bun. She sounds so serious. She's deep in planning mode. I pour myself a cup of black coffee, kiss her head, and sit down beside her.

"Ew, you're so sweaty," she frowns.

"Worked out," I say, drinking my coffee.

"I hope you plan on cleaning up before your big date."

I roll my eyes, but the corner of my mouth twitches into a smile that my extremely focused kid doesn't notice. "It's not a date, Dais. It's a meal."

"Why do adults always try to overcomplicate things?" she asks. "Like, seriously, Dad. Who asks somebody they hardly know out to dinner just as friends? You're actually *not* friends. So, it's a date. A weird one with kids, but whatever. You do you, boo boo."

I almost choke on my coffee. "You're thirteen years old," I say. "Shouldn't you be playing video games or something?"

"Oh, I will," she says. "But first, breakfast. I'm feeling omelets."

She turns off her tablet and heads to the fridge. She pulls out all the ingredients and gets to work. The last few days have been a blur of adjusting to the new normal. Buying food was easy. I just let the kids drive the shopping cart and get what they wanted.

But seeing how grown up my girls are has been hard. In the past when they've slept over, we often stayed at the compound and ran out for breakfast to a diner or a donut shop. But I told the kids they need to live their lives like they would if they were with their mom, just with the other parent. I want the transition to feel as close to normal as I can make it. And they've shown me too much about what normal with Shayla was like.

The first night, Holly asked me what time I wanted her to wake me up in the morning.

"Why would you wake me up?" I asked.

She looked at me like I was stupid. "You need to take us to school, Dad. The bus won't pick us up at your house—"

"Our house," I corrected and held up a hand. "I know about the bus, Hols. I'm asking why I would need my daughter to wake my ass up in the morning. I know how to set an alarm."

Holly was silent as she thought about that. "Are you sure you'll get up, though? I mean, if we're late..."

I raked a hand through my hair and tried not to yank it from the roots. "Isn't it normally the parent screaming at the kids to get up and get ready for school on time?"

She shook her head. "No. I don't know."

But I did. I knew exactly what that meant. Just like I got it when, on Friday night, Holly walked into my room and helped herself to my clothing hamper.

"What the hell are you doing?" I asked.

"When do you do laundry?" she asked, looking apologetic.

"Whenever the hell I want to," I say, pointing for her

to set down the basket. "And I do my laundry my damn self."

Holly nodded. "Even towels? I can throw yours in with ours."

"Even towels." I'd growled and taken my basket back from Holly.

Part of me was proud that my kids were so damn capable. Getting themselves up for school, making their own lunches, doing laundry. But this isn't basic shit.

Daisy does almost all the cooking. At thirteen, I still ate cold hot dogs out of the package. At thirteen, my kid makes omelets and salads, burgers and chicken with rice. She's so short she still needs to climb onto the counter to reach the spices she made me buy, yet she's up there right now, pulling out I don't even know what. And I truly don't. What the fuck kind of spice goes into an omelet other than salt?

It took less than a week of living with these kids full-time to see that my daughters spent a hell of a lot of time making sure Shayla's life worked. They're in no sports, no clubs. They don't hang out at their friends' houses or have sleepovers. "Cuz Mom doesn't trust strangers."

I don't know what normal kids should do, but I'm sure as hell not going to let these kids play momma with me.

"Leave it," I say to Daisy, taking the carton of eggs from her hand. "I'll cook."

She wrinkles her nose. "Dad, no disrespect, but are you serious?"

I know I can't cook for shit, so this is one thing I'll

cave on. "All right," I relent, handing her the carton. "I'll go shower."

"Now?" She whirls on me, an accusing look on her face. "Are you going to shower again later? You have a date tonight."

I pinch my brows between two fingers. Daisy is definitely the micromanager of the two, and the last thing I need is my daughter telling me when and how to bathe. But then I catch myself. This is being a dad. Respecting what she says. Listening to her opinions. And besides, she's not wrong.

I lift the bottom of my tee and mop my sweaty face dry, then open my arms for a hug. "Come here," I tell her. "How would I live without your advice? Give your old dad a hug."

"Ew, no. Go shower." She backs toward the stove. "Dad, get away. You're disgusting."

I leave my youngest cooking up some delicious-smelling shit on the stove and head upstairs to my room with a smile on my face. I never expected this full-time dad shit to be easy, but so far, it's fucking awesome. Which makes me feel even more worried about how Shayla is doing without them.

It's noon before Holly stumbles down the stairs, her eyes puffy. She looks exhausted and stressed.

"Hey, kid." I'm reading a text on my phone from Savage, and I am not happy.

"Sorry, Dad." Holly walks over to the fridge and pours herself a huge glass of water.

"For what?" I ask, putting down my phone before I crack it. "What happened?"

She drops into a kitchen chair beside me and cocks her head. "Where's Dais?"

I jerk a thumb toward the sliding glass door that leads from my kitchen to the yard. "Reading outside. She left you a plate in the fridge."

Holly helps herself to the plate, sniffs it, and then puts it in the microwave. "Yum," she says. "I'm starving." She punches the buttons to heat up her food. "I haven't had my own room in like ever. And it's so quiet here. I can't believe I slept this late. Is there anything you need me to do?"

I get up, grab my wallet, and leave some cash on the counter. "Yeah," I tell her. "Be a fucking teenager. Talk on the phone to your friends—except that Tyler asshole. Your girl friends. Play games on your phone. I don't know. Whatever you normally do on a Saturday." I point to the cash. "I don't need you to do a damn thing except enjoy a day off school. Order a pizza or something for lunch if you want it. I'll be back in time for dinner."

"Where are you going? You have a date tonight, remember?" She pops two slices of bread into the toaster and looks at me in warning. "What time is the reservation?"

Now I see what they mean about girls ruling the world. Society could come to an end, and me and Savage, Shadow, even that Tyler shithead, would all be beating one another to a pulp and eating dirt, while women would keep people fed, clean, and getting where they needed to be on time.

"Hols," I say, trying not to sound shitty. "I'm a grown-ass man. I'll be back in time for dinner."

She nods. "Okay. If you want to make a good first impression, though, you might want to be early. Not on time. Like five minutes early. It sends a message." Her toast pops up, and she grabs butter from the fridge. "Oh, and pick up flowers if you have time."

Now, that is actually a good idea. One I wouldn't have thought of.

"Anything else, boss?" I ask.

"Do you mind if we Uber to the mall?" she asks.

I shake my head. "No rideshares by yourself. I'll have one of the guys come and drive you. You need more money?" I peel off another hundred.

She shakes her head. "You don't have to do that, Dad."

I come around the table and grip her shoulders in my hands. "Hols, I'm not an ATM, but this is your first weekend away from your normal schedule. If you want to go to the mall and have some fun, I'm giving you money to do it." I peel off another hundred, but then I freeze. "Is Tyler working today? Is this about a boy?"

Holly looks shocked and then laughs. "Oh my God, Dad. I'm not a stalker. I wanted to pick up some supplies, that's all."

My pulse calms a little. "No boys. I can't go back to prison."

She chuckles. "I'm glad you're doing this, Dad."

"Doing what?"

"This date," she says, loading her eggs onto the toast to make a sandwich. "You've been single as long as I can remember. You should find someone, you know? Not every woman is going to treat you like Mom did."

My breath catches in my throat. "This isn't a date," I tell her, despite what I said when I asked Poppy out. "This is about being…" I don't know what to say. I sure as fuck don't want to tell my fifteen-year-old daughter that I couldn't think of a better way to see the sexy salon owner again. "Grateful. She did right by you girls, and paying the bill was the least she deserved. Dinner is a gesture."

Holly gives me a smug smile. "Okay, Dad. Whatever you say. It's totally not a date because you're not single and Poppy isn't beautiful. Cool. Got it."

"Text me when you need a ride," I grumble, shaking my head.

These girls. They are too damned smart for their own good—or *my* own good.

I shout goodbye to Daisy through the patio doors and hop on my bike. This may be my new normal at home, but it's business as usual at the club. And Daddy's got to go to work.

SEVEN
POPPY

THE ENTIRE RIDE to the restaurant, Jax has been quiet. I assumed he was absorbed in drawing something on his iPad, but when I park the car, he says, "If it sucks, can we leave?"

I turn to face him in the back seat. "If what sucks? Dinner?" I ask. I shouldn't be surprised that Jax has questions or maybe even anxiety about going out tonight. We've never done anything like this before.

He shrugs. "What if it's boring?"

I take a deep breath and nod. "Honey, we're having dinner. That's all. We'll eat and we'll go." I say it to him because it's the same thing I've been telling myself all week. "Are you nervous?"

I ask him the question I haven't dared even to think. Because I am nervous as hell. I changed my outfit six times. The first two skirts seemed too frivolous. Black jeans felt like what I wear to work. The wrap dress I dusted off was flattering but so low-cut, I knew the only thing I'd be able to think about all night was covering my cleavage.

I finally put on a dress I bought eight years ago. I had no idea back then that I'd have no more date nights.

But tonight, I feel pretty and so nervous, I've been fighting the urge to puke all afternoon.

"I'm not nervous," Jax says.

But I'm not convinced.

I reach my hand behind me and squeeze his knee. "We've got this," I tell him. "Come on. We eat, we talk to some nice new people, and we go back home and watch movies. Deal?"

He nods, unbuckles himself, and jumps out, tucking his tablet in the pocket on the back of the seat.

We walk side by side through the parking lot, and I see Phantom standing out front with Holly and Daisy.

My heart catches in my throat at the sight of him. "That's them," I whisper, my hand resting lightly on Jax's back.

Jax's head whips toward me. "That guy? What is he, a superhero? He's huge."

I chuckle, remembering in that minute that my little boy, who happens to love animation and drawing, is still a little boy. Of course he'd think Phantom looks like a comic book hero. Most of the teachers he has are women and out-of-shape middle-aged men. I don't think he's ever seen anyone in real life who looks like Phantom.

I wave, and I watch as Phantom's eyes travel from my hair, down my dress, to my shoes and back.

"Are we late?" I ask. "Have you been waiting long?"

Daisy is the one who answers. "We told our dad it was good date etiquette to get here first." She looks from me to Jax. "Hi, I'm Daisy." She sticks out her hand, and my son dutifully shakes it.

"I'm Jax," he says.

"It's not a..." I start to remind everyone here, especially myself, that this is not a date, when Phantom leans forward, and the words die on my lips.

He leans close to my ear and plants the lightest, airiest kiss against my ear. "You look stunning," he says. Then he pulls back and sticks out his hand. "Jax, if I had a cool name like yours, I wouldn't need a nickname. But since my real name is lame, my friends call me Phantom."

I swear my son's mouth falls open. But he clamps it shut fast and shakes Phantom's hand. "Nice to meet you," he says.

Holly introduces herself to my son, then turns and gives me a warm hug. "You look really beautiful," she says. "Wow. I love your dress."

Before I can answer, Daisy takes charge. "Our tables should be ready. Let's go. Jax, you're with me and Holly."

I throw a look at Phantom, but he looks as confused as I feel.

Daisy is speaking to the hostess, who turns to us with a smile. "Great, you can all follow me."

Phantom lowers one brow and shoots his daughter a look so severe that if he were my dad, I would have peed my pants. But Daisy practically skips in her white

Chucks and orange sundress, following close behind the hostess.

"We weren't sure how old you were, so we brought some stuff to do." Holly opens a large messenger bag, but I can't see what's inside. "You're not six, obviously, so you don't have to color, but we have comics and our iPad. Do you play any games?"

The hostess sets three menus down on one table, and Holly points to a chair for Jax. Daisy waves to her dad with a grin. "Bye. Two tables, one bill. Don't worry, Dad, we know you're paying."

I must have my mouth wide open because I suddenly feel the heat of Phantom's hand hovering close to my lower back. "Your son going to be okay with this?"

I would check with Jax, but he's not even paying attention to me. He's deep in conversation with Daisy, his back to the adults like we're not even there and, in a way, we're not.

"He'll let me know if he's not," I say, shaking my head, a grin climbing over my face.

Phantom pulls out the chair for me, and I step close to him to take my seat, breathing deeply as I pass him.

I take my seat and will myself to focus on the food and not the man. I grab my menu like it's a room divider and hold it between us so I can collect myself. I scan the food and the prices, the drinks, and, again, the prices, my eyes blurring over the menu until everything runs together.

"Poppy?" Phantom's voice breaks through my panic, and I peek at him over the top of my menu.

"Everything okay? Would you feel more comfortable at the kids' table? I swear I didn't know about this."

I look behind me to make sure Jax is okay, but he and Daisy are laughing like they are old friends, while Holly points at the menu and politely places her order with the waitress.

"I'm…" I don't know what to say. I'm not fine. "I'm freaking out," I admit. I drop the menu and meet Phantom's piercing blue eyes. "I haven't done anything like this since my husband died. I'm overwhelmed."

All of a sudden, Phantom reaches a hand across the table and takes mine firmly. "Hey," he says.

He doesn't say more, just holds my hand in his. The heat of his skin melts me, the tingling and warmth making their way up my arm and through my body until I swear I feel my shoulders relax.

"I love this place. Come here a lot. No doubt it's why that little asshole over there took some liberties with the hostess. You drink?" He releases my hand and gestures for the server to come by.

I don't drink—not much anyway, but I just nod.

He orders two drinks by their name, and I have no idea what I'm in for, but I just want to sit back and enjoy this. I don't think, in all the years I was with Michael, he ordered for me.

I breathe in deeply, enjoying the feeling of being taken care of. And I realize once he's ordered that my hand is still stretched out across the table, waiting for Phantom to hold it. I yank it back and adjust the napkin on my lap, then nervously pick up the menu.

Phantom takes it from me and sets it down. "Allergies?" he asks.

I shake my head.

"Anything you hate or love?"

I shake my head again, dazzling myself with my inability to form words.

He nods. "Holly picked up some food allergies as a kid. Nothing serious, but enough that I always think twice now before assuming. I'll order, unless you saw anything that struck you."

I sigh in relief. "That sounds perfect."

I don't know who this woman is. The woman who can't order for herself off a menu. Who wants a total stranger to hold her hand across the table and ease her nerves. But something about Phantom makes me want to give control over to him. It makes no sense. I've cut the hair of plenty of attractive guys in the salon. I've been on a handful of dates over the years. But this man is powerful but gentle.

Phantom is a mystery. One that I can't believe I'm not just falling deeper into, but I'm running toward at full speed.

The waitress returns with two drinks, and as soon as she sets them down, Phantom lifts his to toast.

"To the most beautiful woman I've ever seen agreeing to have dinner with me." Coming from anyone else, I might have rolled my eyes. Coming from Phantom, that line makes heat pool between my legs.

I lift my glass and toast with him, then take a long sip. "Ooh," I say, the alcohol hitting me fast. "That goes down way too easy."

"Let it," he says. "Enjoy it."

He takes a sip of his drink, then points to my ring finger. "That ink for your ex?"

I nod, then trace my finger over the faded heart that sits where my wedding band used to. "I actually got it after he died," I explain. "Michael wasn't a fan of tattoos, and I always wanted one. I figured after he died, he'd probably be okay if the one I got was sort of a tribute to him."

"That ain't a problem I ever had." Phantom grins, shoving the sleeves of his black dress shirt up a little farther. "Probably got my first when I wasn't much older than Holly."

That shocks me. "Wow," I say.

He nods. "My childhood was nothing like what I'm trying to give my girls."

"I don't know," I say, taking another sip of my drink. "I'm not giving Jax the life I dreamed of for him. I try, but I'm tired." I look him in the eye, suddenly not able to hold back. "I've been a single mom for eight years, and I always told myself, it'll get easier when he's older, when he goes to school. And Jax is a great kid, I mean, really great. But doing it alone? It never gets easier. Only different."

Phantom nods. "When you said you were a single mom, I assumed divorce. I'm sorry to hear his old man passed."

"Thank you."

The waitress returns. "Phantom, the girls ordered dessert with their dinner. I'll bring it after they eat their meals, but I assume that's okay with you?"

He nods. "As long as the boy's mom says he can have dessert, it's okay by me."

The waitress looks to me. "Yes, of course," I say. I can't remember the last time I let Jax order dessert. But if I'm ever going to loosen up and live in the moment, this feels like the time to do it.

Phantom places an order for us, and I only half hear him. I'm looking behind us at Jax and the girls, but they seem to be having an incredible time. Maybe this is my sign to do the same. I take another sip of that delicious drink until Phantom's hand crosses the table and takes mine again. He traces his fingers along the faded ink of my tiny tattoo.

"You were saying?" he asks.

If I was saying something, the thoughts fly right out of my hand at the feel of his fingers against mine. I giggle, and I realize that I'd better sip some water and slow my pace on that drink.

"So, what do you do?" I ask, reaching for a neutral topic. As soon as the words are out of my mouth, I remember what my client said about his biker buddies being criminals. "Unless you don't want to talk about it."

A lazy smile curls over his lips, and all I can think about is running my hands through his beard. He's telling me about his club and the businesses they run, but I'm just staring and only half listening. He's staring right back, with that unbelievable intensity that makes me wish we were alone in a room and not two people at a small table surrounded by our kids and a restaurant full of people.

After I have a few more sips of my drink, the waitress puts a plate in front of me, and I take a bite of the most delicious lobster ravioli I've ever eaten. This is officially the best meal I've ever had and the best company I've been with in ages.

"How did you end up doing hair?" Phantom asks, motioning to the waitress for another round of drinks.

I can't stop the smile that covers my face. "Well, if you ask my sister, I was born to do hair." I laugh. "I've always loved makeup and hair. I tried dyeing my hair using real bleach when I was twelve because I heard my mom talking about someone being a bleach blonde." I laugh even harder at the memory. "Of course, that is not how it works."

Phantom's eyes follow my every move, and my skin pebbles under his gaze. "I went to community college for one year after high school, trying to figure out if there was anything else I wanted to do. But in the end, I went to beauty school."

"Why would you go to community college if you knew what you wanted to do?" he asks, studying my face.

I shrug. "Michael, my husband. We were high school sweethearts. He was incredibly ambitious. He really didn't love the idea of me not going to college, of working on my feet all day." Phantom's face falls a bit, but he doesn't say anything, so I go on. "My mom agreed with him, but I ended up doing what I really wanted to do."

"How did you end up with your own place?" He's finished his dinner and is leaning with his elbows on the table, listening like this is the only place on earth he wants to be.

"That's where my life story gets a little tragic." I explain to him that my dad retired from a job he absolutely hated when I got pregnant with Jax. "He wanted to be a hands-on grandpa." I smile and take another sip of my drink to hide my tears. "Dad was incredibly handy. He spent the first year of his retirement building my salon," I say. "He was a bookkeeper his whole life. He didn't have many skills, but he was hell-bent on seeing me be my own boss, have a place where I could pursue my dream and raise my son. He really wanted me to have it all. And since Clara went to beauty school too, he figured building the business was something he could give to both his girls."

"Why do I get the feeling there's not a happy ending to this story?" Phantom asks, his hand finding mine across the table again. I can't believe I don't even think about pulling away.

"Because there's not," I say, looking down. "Dad died just after the salon opened. He worked his whole life doing something he hated, spent one year of retirement putting his blood, sweat, and tears into my salon, and then, he died. Massive heart attack. Mom found him at home, but he'd been gone at least a couple of hours. There was nothing that could be done."

I use the hand that Phantom isn't holding to take another sip of my drink. This poor man. This has to be the worst date he's ever had. Between talking about my dead husband and my dead father.

"I'm sorry you've been through so much. You're one hell of a strong woman."

I chuckle. "It sure doesn't feel like it most of the time," I say. "But thank you."

He's looking at me, his eyes following my lips as I speak. The table feels suddenly very small, and when I cross my legs, I accidentally kick his shin under the table.

"Oops, sorry," I say.

His face is composed, his shoulders relaxed. His hand is still on mine, our knees so close under the table, I swear I feel his heat through his jeans. I think I need to get up and use the restroom. Splash some water on my face and clear my mind. Check on Jax. Put some distance between this gorgeous man and thoughts that can't lead me anyplace good.

I pull my hand from his. "Will you excuse me... Whoa."

When I stand, the full impact of the drink makes itself known. "Uh-oh," I say. "It's been way too long since I've had a drink that strong. I think I'm going to need to call a taxi to get home. I'm feeling a little too buzzed to drive."

Phantom is on his feet in an instant. He stands beside me and helps me out of my chair. "Fuck that," he says. "I'll get you and your car home. Are you all right? You need some air?"

I giggle despite myself. "I'm actually amazing," I tell him, realizing that my inhibitions are a little too far gone, thanks to the alcohol. But damn it all, I'm going with it. "This has been the best dinner of my life," I say.

"I'm having a great time. Too good, actually. I want to check on Jax and use the ladies' room. Before I say or do anything that I'll regret when the drinks wear off."

Phantom's smile reaches from his beautiful lips to his midnight-blue eyes. "I'll take you."

He presses a hand against my lower back, and we stop at the kids' table on the way.

"Baby," I say, but then regret calling him that in front of the girls. "Jax, I mean, how is your dinner?"

"Amazing, Mom. Are we going already?" Jax's cheeks are flushed, and the table is covered with comic books, coloring books and colored pencils, and the girls' tablets.

I stroke Jax's shoulder. "No, I'm only going to the ladies' room. Just checking in on you all."

"We're good," Daisy says. "Just waiting for dessert."

Phantom kisses his daughter's head and nods at Jax, before walking me toward the back of the restaurant.

"I'll wait here," he says.

I turn toward him, feeling warm and full, a little buzzed and happy. Without even thinking, I reach out and cup his cheek, letting my fingers stroke his beard. "You are amazing. Not like anyone I've ever met," I murmur, fluttering my eyes closed and breathing in his warm scent. "What are you?"

He growls my name, a low and hungry sound. "Poppy…" He snakes a hand behind my hair and pulls me against him, his sweet breath soft against my cheeks. "I'm a man who hopes this isn't our only date."

I look up into his eyes, and my body goes liquid. I want to lean against him, crash my body into his. God, I want to taste him. I am about to kiss this man. This man who's a near stranger to me. It wouldn't be the first kiss I've had since losing Michael, but close enough to it that I realize how stupid that would be of me.

I snap my head back and shake it lightly, willing myself to sober up. "I'd better go," I say, backing away on wobbly legs.

I rush into the ladies' room, take care of business, and then splash some cold water on my face. I look in the mirror and smooth down my hair. I'm okay, I tell myself. I haven't done anything wrong or stupid. No matter how attracted I am to him, no matter how complicated this feels, I'm not doing anything wrong.

I want more.

I don't know what this means, but I'm hoping with all my heart and some very inappropriate parts of my body that Phantom meant what he said.

EIGHT
PHANTOM

IF I THOUGHT a family date would be easy, simple, I was dead wrong.

During the entire meal, I could hardly keep my hands to myself. I wanted to touch every bit of Poppy's exposed skin. I'd developed an unhealthy obsession with her bare shoulder, and I'm cursing the fact that the dress she's got on isn't strapless. Hell, what I wouldn't give for a full view of this woman.

She's gorgeous and fragile. She's honest in a way that too many people aren't. And I don't mean women I've dated. They tend to be brutally honest about what they want: money, someone to fuck, and usually someone to take care of them.

Poppy is different. I feel like she wants me every bit as much as I want her. But she's fighting it. Trapped in an old love story with a husband who's a ghost.

The only question is how long it's going to take for Poppy to be ready. Because when it happens, when I make her mine, there won't be any room for ghosts between us.

Savage and Shadow show up right after I get the bill paid. I load Poppy and all the kids into my truck, and Shadow follows us in Poppy's car, so she doesn't have to worry about getting back to her place safely. After we figure out who's driving where, we head out.

The drive to Poppy's is rowdy. The three kids sit together in the back seat, cracking one another up and talking like they've known one another all their lives.

Jax is a whip-smart kid with a great sense of humor. I can tell by the way Daisy talks to him that he's probably not going to be a candidate for her future babysitting business. They sound more like best friends. I'm just glad they're paying attention to each other so I can enjoy the last few minutes of Poppy's company.

"I meant what I said in the restaurant," I say, flicking a look at her.

She's staring straight ahead, but I can see the corner of her mouth turn into a smile. "Me too," she says quietly. "I'm right there," Poppy says, pointing. But as we pull into the driveway, she leans all the way forward in the seat. "Something's wrong," she says, her voice low. "Phantom, is the front door open? My front light is off. I never leave it off."

I jump out of the truck and come around to the passenger side. I open the door and pop the glove box in front of Poppy's lap. I meet her eyes and keep my voice calm as I grab my Glock. "Stay here and keep the kids quiet," I tell her, resting a hand on her knee. "I'll send Shadow to sit with you."

Her eyes go huge when she sees my gun, but she nods and turns to the kids. I close the passenger door, then jog down to the driveway and motion for Savage to get out. I point to the front door. Shadow joins me, already pulling out his piece, but I motion with a finger toward my truck with the kids and Poppy.

Savage approaches the front door like a SEAL about to breach an enemy camp. He nudges the door open quietly with his elbow, something he does so he doesn't leave boot prints on the door. Then he enters, his weapon drawn, without making a sound. I follow, looking back to see Shadow behind the wheel of my truck, watching the whole thing go down.

My heart hammers in my throat, and my adrenaline kicks into high gear as we step through mountains of shit on the floor. Papers are shredded and tossed everywhere. The couch is turned over, the television is smashed. Even if Poppy were a hoarder, there's no way she lives with her place looking like this.

Something is very, very wrong here. Somebody trashed Poppy's place.

Savage motions to me, and we go through the living room to a small, open kitchen. The fridge is hanging wide open, and every condiment that was once inside has been shattered on the floor. Glass and food coat the walls and the floor. We don't touch anything and back up, careful not to disturb anything. We don't turn on any lights and use only the flashlights on our phones to survey the damage.

I head down a hall and check out a small bathroom and what must be Poppy's bedroom, and then, together, we go upstairs. The house feels still and silent, so I'm guessing whoever was here is long gone.

Nothing upstairs in Jax's room looks disturbed, so we head back down to the living room and make a plan.

"Take all the kids, including Jax, back to my place. I'm going to stay here and wait with Poppy while she calls the cops. The kids don't need to be here for that."

Savage nods. "What the fuck is this?" he asks.

I shake my head. "Whoever did this is dead," I tell him through gritted teeth. "Put the word out. If this is some random break-in, a junkie or a neighborhood thug, I want a name by morning."

He nods. "I know what to do."

We head outside and motion for Shadow to come out and talk to us. I send him back to the compound in Savage's truck and have him leave Poppy's for me to drive later. Then I go around to the passenger side.

Poppy reaches for my arm, her arms wide and her lips parted. "What happened?" she asks quietly. "Is everything okay?"

"It's all clear in there, but you're going to need a cleanup crew," I say loudly for the kids' benefit. "Kids, you want to have Jax and Poppy for a sleepover till we can get their place fixed up?"

Poppy looks furious, terrified, confused. Every emotion races across her face, but she doesn't say anything. Just looks at me, her eyes filled with fear.

I take her hand. "Come on, let me show you what's up, and we'll make a few calls while Savage gets the kids settled."

I take her hand and help her out of the truck, closing the door behind her so the kids can't hear. "Poppy, someone ransacked the shit out of your house," I say, holding both her hands in mine.

"What?" she looks toward the house, but I keep her in place.

"We need to call the cops. You're not going to be able to stay here. I'm going to have Savage get the kids to my place, and you can all crash with me for the night."

"Ransacked?" she echoes, sounding confused. "Like robbed? I don't understand."

"Let's let the kids get out of here and call the police. When the cops are done, I'll help you get what you need, and then we'll get the hell out of here. You with me?"

She nods but doesn't move.

"Poppy," I say gently.

She looks up at me, a shimmer of tears wetting her lashes. "Who?" she asks. "Who did this…"

I shake my head and stifle the urge to pull her to my chest. Not in front of the kids. I'll have time to take care of her once we get the kids to safety.

I take both of her hands in mine and lace our fingers together. "Hey," I say, my voice low. I meet her eyes. "I'm here, and I'm not leaving you. I'm going to take care of this and make damn sure nothing like this ever happens again. You got that?"

She searches my face, and all traces of the happy, buzzed Poppy disappear. Her lips go thin as she presses them together, like she's trying to hold back tears.

"Okay," she finally says. "But I don't want to tell Jax anything until I see for myself."

I nod and release her hands.

She turns and opens the door, putting on a bright smile for Jax. "Honey, are you all right going home with Daisy and Holly? Do you want me to call Grandma or Auntie Clara? We have a little problem with the house, and I'm going to stay here and see how long it's going to take before we can get it fixed."

Jax looks from his mom to me. "Mom, you're coming, right? What happened to the house?"

"I want to go inside and see what's going on. I'm not going to be able to get anyone out tonight to fix it, so we'll stay someplace tonight together. But I can call Grandma if you'd rather go there."

"Come home with us," Daisy says. "My dad's place is so cool."

Jax brightens. "Can we stay up and watch movies until you get there?" he asks.

"We get to stay up until eleven on weekends," Daisy adds helpfully. "And it's only nine now, so we have plenty of time to watch at least one movie and maybe even two if we can stay up late. It *is* a special occasion."

I roll my eyes. I'm going to have my hands full with this girl.

But Poppy nods, then as if she's having second thoughts, she turns to me. "This is too much to ask of you. Why don't I call my mother and…"

"If that's what you want. But you might feel different when you see what's going on in there." I put a hand on her shoulder and lean close to her ear. "I get that we hardly know each other. I wouldn't send my kid off with a stranger either. Savage is ex-military. He's my right hand. I trust the guys with my daughters' lives. You can trust him. You can trust me. The call is yours. You want to go inside and see first, then decide?"

She only hesitates a second. "If the choice is you or my mom, I choose you."

She turns back to the car to address the girls. "Text me as soon as you get there, okay? I'm going to send you my number now. You too." She points at Savage, all traces of her relaxed buzz gone. "Send me the address of where you're going, and let me know when the kids are inside safe."

"Will do," Savage says. "You need anything, you need me to come back here, you say the word. Otherwise, I won't leave the kids until you're there."

We exchange a flurry of texts, and then finally, Savage takes off, leaving just Poppy and me. Then I take her hand. "Come on," I say. "You're going to need to see this."

It takes just under two hours for the police to respond and to complete their preliminary walk-through of the scene. They give her the usual bullshit. Since nothing obvious was stolen, it looks like someone was on the hunt for something. Turns out, Poppy had nothing of value. Even her television was old, and the cops suspected that whoever broke in was pissed they didn't find anything and trashed the place instead.

"Since they didn't seem to go upstairs to your son's room, they might have been interrupted, or they just gave up." The police finish their paperwork, and Officer Callahan extends a hand to me.

"We rarely catch the guys responsible for stuff like this. And since nothing was stolen, they probably won't leave a trail trying to move stolen goods. But we'll let you know if any leads turn up."

I shake the cop's hand and pretend we don't know each other. Pretend that I haven't passed money and other shit to him countless times over the years. Pretend that there is such a thing as a good guy and a criminal—him being the first and me being the shithead. I know how everything works in this town, and Callahan knows I'll get this solved and sorted before he and the night crew pick up coffee and donuts on their next shift.

If I want justice, then I'm going to have to take it myself. He knows it, and I know it. Poppy, however, doesn't understand any of this.

As the cops roll out, silent tears streak down Poppy's face. Her shoulders are hunched, the bare one that peeks out from the cutout in her dress soft and hot under my touch.

"Hey." I turn her to face me, and she looks into my face, her cheeks wet with tears.

"I'm such a fool," she says, shaking her head. "All these years, I've lived alone with my son. I never go anywhere but work. Never do anything. The one night I go out, this happens. Someone was in my house. How can I ever feel safe here again? How can I keep my son safe if I'm terrified?"

I open my arms, and she doesn't hesitate. She moves against my chest, and I hold her. I feel the wet tears stain my shirt, the anger inside me rising to a boil.

"Babe," I say, not able to hold back the word. I think I've known from the moment I set eyes on Poppy that I wanted her. Wanted to make her mine. And whether it becomes more than this or not, she's mine to protect right now.

I lean back and cup her face with my hands. I wipe away her tears with my thumbs, and I lower my head to look deep into those devastated brown eyes. "I'm going to find out who did this, and I'm going to make sure nothing like this ever happens again. Do you understand me? I'm going to keep you and your boy safe."

She sniffles and stares into my eyes, her lips parting softly. "Why?" she whispers. "Why do you want to help us?"

I won't answer that. Because what I want to say will scare this gorgeous woman away, and the only thing I want is to bring her close.

I say nothing as my thumb moves from her cheek to her lower lip. I stroke the bottom edge, and my cock twitches when she gasps and flutters her eyes closed in response.

"Poppy," I breathe, my dick going hard and my pulse thundering in my throat. "You helped me. A fuckload more than I could repay with one dinner."

She opens her eyes and licks her lower lip, almost catching my finger. Heat flashes in her eyes, and for a second, one excruciating second, I think she might kiss me. But as soon as I see it, it's passed.

"I've never felt like this," she says, stumbling away from me and wobbling on her heels.

I don't know if it's the drinks, the fear, or something else, but she goes pale suddenly.

"Phantom..." she says.

I see her knees buckle, and I catch her before she goes down. I scoop her up in my arms and hold her against my chest. "There's nothing you need from inside?" I ask.

"It's all ruined," she says weakly. "There's nothing left except Jax's things."

I say no more and balance her in my arms before setting her carefully back on the passenger seat of her car. I whip out my phone and shoot off a series of texts. Within an hour, this place will be crawling with my brothers. They'll clean the mess and pack up Jax's room and bring everything to my place.

Until we catch whoever the fuck did this, I'm not letting Poppy or her son out of my sight. And when I catch them, the motherfucker who did this is going to pay.

NINE
POPPY

I THINK I'm in shock. That's the only thing that makes sense. I let Phantom hold me, wipe away my tears, and then pick me up and carry me to my car.

I don't even know who I am right now, but in some ways, that's a good thing. I don't want to be a woman who is experienced in this kind of situation. The break-in, the police.

So many things in my life changed the night we lost Michael, and my sense of safety in this world, the bubble I've created for Jax and me, just popped.

We don't speak during the drive, but Phantom's fingers are laced tightly through mine. He doesn't let go, and I don't want him to. I'm already growing used to the rough feel of his skin, the size, heat, and strength of his hands.

I'm a mess, but if I have to go through this, is it really so wrong to accept help? What makes me most worried isn't just the fact that I am accepting help from this man I hardly know, but the fact that I'm liking it.

I'm not used to leaning on anyone anymore. I thought I'd been through it all in the last eight years, but this... This is uncharted territory.

I watch Phantom as he stares straight ahead, steering with his left hand while he holds mine with his right.

His lips twist as if he's muttering curses under his breath, and wrinkles form around his eyes as he glares. I feel like he's as angry for me as I am, and something about that makes me feel better. He's not just doing this for me. He's going through this with me.

I look away and stare out the window, trying to make sense of how I got here. But the gorgeous view distracts me. I recognize the neighborhood as we make the fifteen-minute drive from my side of town toward an area I never even dreamed I could afford.

When we pull into the driveway, my breath catches in my chest. My house is a run-down but well-maintained little place. But his place is an absolute fantasy.

While Phantom gets out of the car and rushes around to my side, I look at the two-story glass-and-concrete structure. The home has a mid-century vibe to it, with sharp angles and big windows.

"This is your home?" I ask, marveling again at who this man is. "It's stunning, Phantom."

"And yours for now too. Come on." He holds his hand out to me and, feeling steadier, I take it, but then I release it. I'm getting way too comfortable holding on to this man.

He punches in a code, and the garage door opens to

reveal the motorcycle I saw him on the other day. The garage is perfectly organized and neat, with tools and equipment lined up on shelves on one side and an impressive home gym setup on the side opposite where the bike is parked.

He motions me inside, closes the garage, then unlocks the door that leads into the house.

"Dais. Hols. Jax. We're home."

He nods at me, and I walk inside before him. We enter into a really nice mudroom, where Phantom kicks off his boots. I toe off my shoes and follow him barefoot into a massive living room with sliding glass doors that overlook a large lawn and a dock out back. The three kids are sprawled out on blankets and sleeping bags on the floor, watching a very loud action movie on a huge flat-screen television.

"Yo!" Phantom shouts over the noise.

Holly jumps up and reaches for the remote, then cranks the volume down a few notches. "Hey, Dad. Savage is in the kitchen."

Daisy scrambles up from her bright-purple sleeping bag and crashes into her dad for a hug. "Can we finish the movie, Dad, please? It's like twenty more minutes."

Jax comes over to me and gives me a hug. I have no words. I just hold him close and breathe in the familiar scent of his hair. "Hey, baby." It's all I can manage. Thankfully, Jax fills in the silence for me.

"Mom, this movie is the one we were going to watch together, but I didn't think you'd mind." He looks up at me apologetically. "Is it okay?"

I nod. "Of course, honey. It's fine. Are you having fun?"

"Yeah," he says, and he does sound happy. His shoes are off, but he's still wearing his dress pants and shirt. I didn't even think to grab him a toothbrush or pajamas. My stomach sinks at what a shitty mom I am, but then Holly is at my elbow.

"We don't have any boy clothes, but I pulled out some basketball shorts with laces and a T-shirt from my dad's closet." She motions to Phantom. "Dad, you had like three new toothbrushes in the bathroom vanity, so I set two out for Jax and Poppy."

Phantom nods. "You mind finding Poppy something to change into? I want to talk to Savage."

Holly jumps up and is about to head upstairs, but I stop her. "It's all right. Finish your movie, honey. I'm just going to sit a minute."

Holly looks to her dad, who nods, and then she gives me a smile. "Okay, we moved all the furniture around when Daisy and I moved in, so there's a guest bedroom upstairs with twin beds. I'll grab you some clothes before we go to sleep."

I nod, and Phantom comes beside me.

While the kids turn the volume back up on their movie, Phantom leans close to my ear. "I'll be right back. You want a drink or something? Water?"

"Water would be great." I turn to follow him, and he holds up his hand as if to stop me, but then he seems to think better of it.

We head into the kitchen, where the blare of the movie masks Savage's low voice. He nods at me.

"Who responded?" Savage asks.

"Callahan." Phantom's eyes never leave his phone.

"Good," Savage says. "I got King and two other prospects over at the house now. Viper's supervising."

"King," I mumble to myself. "Prospects?"

Savage smirks. "Phantom will fill you in later."

They talk about contacts, and then they trade looks. Phantom fills a glass of cold, filtered water from a pitcher in the fridge, and then he hands it to me.

"Poppy." His voice is edged in something I can't identify. "Do you have any idea who'd want to do this to you? Do you have any enemies?"

I feel my knees wobble again, and I lean back against the cool granite countertop. I take a long sip of water, then shake my head. I rub my forehead, pinching my eyebrows together. Between the drinks and the stress of tonight, I've got a killer headache taking shape.

"Do you mind if I sit?" I motion toward a wooden kitchen table with four chairs around it.

Phantom is at my elbow in a heartbeat, taking my glass and leading me to a chair. He leans forward, his eyes dark as midnight. "It's all right," he says. "Take your time."

I swallow back more cold water and grip the glass to keep my hands from shaking. "My mother is Lori Davis," I explain.

"County Commissioner Davis?" Phantom asks, as though he's heard of her.

I'm surprised, but I probably shouldn't be. Our county board is a small organization. The commissioners are elected, but Mom has not had an opponent in over a decade. The position isn't one of any real power, but the county board does have oversight into some country programs and funding. Mom's personal passion is safety and public welfare.

She's served on the parole board, parent-teacher association, the library board, and contributes to just about any community enrichment program you can imagine. Take Back the Night walks. Cookie sales. My mother is the reason we have security lights and cameras in all the privately owned commercial spaces. The reason I have a timer on the lights at my house. Although I deluded myself into thinking in a town this small I wouldn't need one, and I'm regretting that decision now.

Even worse, the fact that Lori Davis's daughter's house was broken into will be big news in this small city. That's why the first call I made tonight was not to my mother. What happened at my house won't just be personal for Mom.

I nod. "I kept my married last name after Michael died so Jax and I would have the same last name. Easier for school registration and everything."

"Does your mom have enemies?" Savage asks. "The commissioners don't do much but plan parades and make sure the senior center's pancake breakfast stays on budget."

Phantom shoots his friend a lethal look, and Savage goes quiet.

"That's not exactly true," I say. "I mean, Mom takes the job seriously, but you're right. It's not like she has political enemies." Now, Michael, on the other hand... I open my mouth to say something, but it seems ridiculous even now.

My husband's death was ruled an accident. Even after the insurance company hired someone to prove there was no way Michael could have slid off that bridge and sustained the damage to his car that he did, in the end, the police closed the case. There was no one to go after. No reason to do anything but accept the reality that my husband was gone.

"Poppy, if there is anything else I should know about..." Phantom's voice is low, and the protectiveness of his hand on my knee sends the tiny hairs on my arms to attention. "Anyone who could be behind this."

He tightens his fingers around my knee when he says "anyone." The thin fabric of my dress separates his hand from my bare skin.

I've always been able to take care of myself and my son, but this is too much. Who's ever prepared for the kind of mess that someone left in my house?

I rally my courage and meet Phantom's eyes. If he's going to help me, I want to be honest. Could there be any connection between my husband's accident and this? There can't be, but I don't want to hold anything back.

"There was a concern when Michael died that he might have been run off the road intentionally. An investigation was done, and the police determined that it was just a terrible accident. I can't imagine that anyone would wait eight years if they have some kind of grudge against my family. That wouldn't make sense.

Nothing's changed. I live in the same house. Nothing about my life is new."

Nothing except my totally irresponsible attraction to this man.

He listens intently, his eyes following my lips as I speak. I look down at his hand on my knee, and he slowly pulls it back.

Phantom practically leaps from the chair and is on the phone before I know what's happening. He barks orders to someone called Hawk and then points at Savage. "Round-the-clock surveillance," he says. "You see anything, you tell me before you stop and take a piss break. We clear?"

Savage grins, and the look on his face is, well, savage. "Crystal. I'll get the word out. We'll find the fucker behind this."

Savage claps Phantom on the back and then leaves. I hear him yell goodbye to the girls just as the credits of the movie start playing.

"Sounds like bedtime," Phantom says, jerking a thumb toward the living room. "Come on. Let's get you and your boy set up."

"Phantom…" I stand up and put my glass in the sink, then shake my head and stare down at my hands. "I can't stay here. I can't impose like that. I'm not your problem. I'm totally sober now, and I can just take Jax and check in to a hotel for the night. Tomorrow, we'll go to my mom's, and…"

He's standing between me and the living room, but I don't feel trapped. Instead, I feel safe. His body is a wall between me and anything out there that might hurt me.

I hate that I feel so drawn to him. Yes, I'm weak right now. I know that, but I have had to be strong for so, so long. I don't want to leave, but it's the right thing to do. To stand up on my own two feet and get my son and myself to safety.

Before I can say another word, he lifts my chin until my eyes meet his. Those beautiful midnight-blue eyes flash with something I wish I understood. "Poppy." His voice is low, and the growl underneath my name makes my belly flip.

I lick my lips and swallow nervously.

"Poppy." This time, my name ends in a groan that betrays the same powerful attraction to me that I can't deny I'm feeling for him.

I flutter my eyes closed so he can't bewitch me with those eyes. "Phantom."

He lowers his lips to my ear and whispers against my hair. "Stay with me," he says. "Let me make sure you and your son are safe. I want you here until I sort this shit out. You can go home as soon as you tell me that's what you want." I feel him reach out and stroke one of the long curls that hangs over my bare shoulder. His fingers just barely touch my skin, and I suck in a shocked breath.

This man.

His touch.

My God, it's electric.

Everything about him.

I open my eyes and lift my face to him, and before I can talk myself out of it, I lean forward. I place the fastest, softest kiss on the corner of his mouth. I get more beard than lip, but it's still the most erotic kiss I think I've ever had. I pull back so slowly, I almost think I'm not moving.

Phantom groans for real then, a strangled sound that sends a flood of wetness between my legs. "Poppy, fuck." He slides his hand beneath my hair, cups my neck, and pulls my mouth to his. "I have wanted to kiss you since the day I met you."

"All that time?" I ask, my heart pounding so hard in my chest I'm sure he can hear it. "One whole week?"

"Every goddamn second. Feels like a year, not a week."

He flicks the tip of his tongue against my lower lip, and I swear my knees buckle.

"Stay with me," he whispers. "Every single thing you want is yours. You want space, I'll give you space. You want to go home, I'll respect that, once the place is clean enough for you to move back in." He threads his long fingers through the back of my hair and tugs lightly. "You want me," he murmurs, kissing my lips in light, flicking kisses between each word, "I'm all fucking yours, baby."

My eyes fly open, and I realize my son and his daughters are just a few feet away, probably ready to burst into the kitchen any minute and catch their parents in some highly un-first-date-like behavior. Although, now that I think about it, how would I know anymore what people do on first dates? Maybe a little light kissing in the kitchen is normal.

"I should get Jax," I say, even though every part of my body wants more of Phantom. Could I ever handle a man like him? I'm not sure I can even manage a night under the same roof. I throw my shoulders back, and Phantom's eyes fly to my very obviously hard nipples. So much for being able to go braless in this dress.

I cross my arms over my chest as a hot blush sears its way up my neck and cheeks.

"Fuck me," Phantom groans, closing his eyes, his head dropping back. He shakes out his shoulders and adjusts his jeans a bit, making me think the bulge in the front of his jeans means he's as turned on as I am. "Bedtime. Sleep, I mean. The kids. Fuck." He lets out a frustrated sigh. "Let's get everybody tucked in."

He turns and stalks out of the kitchen, and I follow close behind, wondering what the heck I think I'm doing. I hardly know this man. He hardly knows me.

The police said they won't be able to find whoever did this. What makes Phantom think he can, and what will he do with them if he does?

I start to think about the things my client said about the bikers when Phantom showed up at my shop on his bike wearing his leather vest. Are these guys criminals? It's hard to believe the hands that fisted my hair and touched my hands so perfectly could be used to hurt someone.

As I follow Phantom, Holly, and Daisy up the stairs toward the guest room, my hand on Jax's shoulder, I wonder, after everything I've been through, if Phantom is the hero I never knew I needed, or if he's the exact kind of danger I've been avoiding for all these years.

TEN

PHANTOM

IT TAKES every shred of strength I possess to leave Poppy behind. I loaned her an old shirt and a pair of my boxers to sleep in, and after she'd changed for bed and brushed her teeth, all I could look at was the swell of her large, perfect tits underneath my shirt. If it weren't for the boy, even with my daughters here, it would have required every ounce of my will to keep myself from scooping her into my arms and taking even more than what she offered me in the kitchen.

There will be time for that later.

I'll make sure of it.

For now, I need to know whose life I'm going to end.

Once everyone is tucked away, I arm the house and check the camera feed to my phone. Satisfied that nothing will go down here without my knowing about it, I text Hawk to come keep watch until I get back, and I text Dylan aka Jizz to make sure he's working at Poppy's on cleanup. Then I head down to the garage, let myself out, and get behind the wheel of my truck.

I drive to the compound with the wheels spinning so fast, I can't keep the anger and fear separate. If there's nothing in Poppy's life that led to this, maybe it was random. Could've been anybody casing the house who just happened to notice that the people who are always home actually weren't.

I hope that's what happened.

What's going to be harder to do is face the one person I stopped calling for help years ago.

By the time I storm into the club, the party is in full swing. Blade's sitting in a recliner, his head thrown back and his cock in Stella's mouth. They both must be really, really fucked up because Stella and Blade are friends. Not fuck buddies like most of the bitches who hang around here.

I look away from what appears to be Stella giving a decent blow job and scan the crowd for Shadow. He's got himself an old lady, so he's the only one not fucking or trying to get himself fucked here tonight.

Penny and a new girl whose name I can never remember are both topless, their tits out while they play strip poker with Viper and a prospect who's also missing half of his clothes. I smell weed and sweat, piss and the heavy scent of cigarette smoke.

As soon as I see the prospect here at the compound and not at Poppy's house, my vision goes red. I storm over to the recliner and grab Dylan's vest, yanking him up and out of the chair so hard the bitch on his cock falls off and tumbles onto the floor.

"What the fuck?" she screams, her eyes red.

"What the fuck are you doing here?" I point to her.

"You fucking him? He's not supposed to be here, so unless you're going to fuck somebody else tonight, you better get the fuck out of here."

Dylan looks stunned, but he's zipping his pants and wiping his mouth. "Phantom, fuck, I…"

I grab him with both hands, lift him off the floor, and throw him into a wall. "Where the fuck you supposed to be, prospect?"

The entire compound goes silent except for the music, which someone turns off once it's clear the party is over.

Dylan crumples against the floor and covers his face like he expects me to hit him.

I bend down, pick his ass up by the shirt, and again shove him into the wall. But this time, I lean so close to him I can smell the sweet stink of something on his breath.

"I don't care what you snort, smoke, or suck," I seethe into his face, "as long as you're never so out of control that you can't do your job. Now what the fuck were you doing here? Because fucking that bitch is not your fucking job. And if I have to remind you what your fucking job is…"

"No." Dylan's whole body starts shaking. "I'm sorry, Phantom. I'm sorry. I left Jasper at that lady's house. He—"

"I don't remember telling you that you could delegate the job I gave you. Have I gone fucking senile and forgot what I told you to do?"

Dylan shakes his head even faster than the rest of him is trembling.

Viper is by my side in a second. "I got this." Viper's voice is ice-cold, and I'm damned sure that Dylan pisses his pants. He's lucky he's not pissing blood right now.

I nod at Shadow, who's leaning against the bar drinking a beer. "My office."

He nods.

"Turn the fucking music back on!" I shout, and the music picks back up. The party resumes—except, of course, for Dylan. I don't envy the lesson Viper's about to teach him.

I walk through the crowd, dodging pool sticks and limbs with Shadow close behind.

"Fuck that kid," I seethe.

"Fuck that kid," Shadow agrees. "I made some calls. You want news on the break-in?"

"It was her, wasn't it?" I grit out, my hands in fists. "Tell me you got eyes on Shayla and she wasn't involved in this." I don't think my blood pressure can take any more tonight.

"I got eyes on her," Shadow confirms. "Drove past her place myself. She was home. Lights on. I could see her through the window. Doesn't mean she didn't have something to do with this, though."

A sick feeling settles in my gut. My ex-wife knows better than to target me or my house or my kids.

There's no way Shayla knows my lawyer has a statement from Poppy. Which means the only thing Shayla knows is that I found out she tried to rip Poppy off. She probably assumes Poppy ratted her out to me so I'd pay the bill, and she's pissed enough to take it out on someone. Poppy is the most obvious target. Shayla knows what will happen if she comes anywhere near me, the compound, or our kids.

Shadow is ten steps ahead of me. "If Shayla is behind this... Once she finds out that Poppy wrote a statement to the judge about what happened..." he says, his lips a thin line.

I tear a hand that's shaking with unspent rage through my hair. He doesn't have to say it. I know what this means. Poppy could be in very real danger.

I can't let that happen. If my shitty ex-wife is behind what happened tonight ... Whether she did it herself or got some crackhead boyfriend to do it, I'll protect Poppy until Shayla is behind bars, paying for what she did. And I don't say that lightly.

"If she did this, I swear to fucking God, she's going to pay." I pick up a soft stress ball Holly gave me for Christmas this year that's sitting on the top of my desk and squeeze it, but the goddamn thing doesn't bring even an ounce of relief. I whip it angrily against the wall, where it hits with a thud.

"One step at a time," Shadow reminds me. "We got eyes and ears all over the county. It might take a day or two, but we'll get a name. But, Phantom..." He hesitates, lifting one brow in question. "What're we going to do if Shayla's behind this?"

"You're going to leave that to me." I say it a little too quickly. "Only me. You got that?"

He nods. "You sure? You know how Shayla gets—"

I hold up a hand and glare. I know better than anyone how Shayla gets. That's how I know that I'm the only one who can be trusted to handle this.

"Leave Shayla to me," I grit out. "Get me evidence, and then get the fuck out of the way."

Shadow nods, then heads back toward the party. I drop down in my chair, but the muffled sounds of music and laughter make it impossible to think.

I don't know at this point what I hope for more—that she is behind the break-in at Poppy's or that she had nothing to do with it at all.

ELEVEN
POPPY

I WAKE up the next morning and stretch my arms over my head. Sunlight floods the room, but it's muted, thanks to a privacy tinting that covers the window glass. I roll over in the twin bed, expecting to see Jax across the room from me, but the bed is empty. The blankets are tossed back, and the pillow is all scrunched up into a C-shape—a sure sign that Jax slept here not long ago. But waking up in a strange place and not seeing my son sends my heart into an immediate panic.

I leap out of bed, not caring that I'm braless and wearing Phantom's boxer shorts. I tear down the stairs, only stopping when I hear the sound of Jax's laughter, with Daisy and Holly talking over him.

"They're called mock-mosas," Daisy is saying in a very grown-up voice. "No alcohol, just orange juice and sparkling grape juice. Kid-friendly. Dad approved."

"That's a lotta sugar, Dais." When I hear Phantom's booming voice, I freeze on the stairs. It's hard to explain the feeling that floods my body at the idea of my son hanging out with Phantom and his daughters.

Once I know that Jax is here and he sounds more than okay, I turn around, pad back upstairs, and take care of business in the bathroom. I open the toothbrush the girls left out for me, brush my teeth, and run my fingers through my hair.

After I clean up a little, I head back to the guest room and see a long-sleeved button-down and a pair of sweats outside the door. I throw the loose sweats on over the boxers I'm wearing and tie the button-down around the T-shirt. The outfit will do, considering I still don't have a bra.

As I head back downstairs in Phantom's clothes and my bare feet, an even more uncomfortable feeling overcomes me.

I stand outside the kitchen for a few minutes, listening to laughter and chatter. My son's voice mixes in with Holly's and Daisy's. I don't know what they are doing, but it sounds like fun. The kind of fun I don't think Jax and I have had in a long time.

The ache of longing in my chest is so intense, I lose my breath for a second. I hardly know Phantom, but this feels real, and I want to be a part of it. Not on the outside looking in.

"Mom—" Jax gives me a grin and holds up a glass "—want a mock-mosa?"

"Sounds delicious," I say. The rush of emotions or maybe the drinks I had last night have made the beginning of a headache form behind my eyes. "Water would be good too," I add.

Phantom turns from the counter and meets my eyes. He's holding a cup of coffee and a bottle of Advil. A sexy grin curls one corner of his mouth, and in a flash, I'm back to last night. My kiss on the corner of those perfect lips. The bristles of his dark beard. God, this man...

He crosses the kitchen, his feet bare, well-broken-in jeans low on his hips, and a soft gray T-shirt clinging to his sculpted chest. "Mornin'," he whispers, offering me the coffee and the painkillers. "A little something for the morning after."

I groan and accept them both gratefully. "How long have you all been up?"

Phantom shakes his head. "Doesn't matter. It's Sunday. A day off. We sleep when we want, we eat what we want..."

"And we drink mock-mosas." Daisy hands me a glass filled to the brim. "Sparkling grape juice and orange juice," she says. "So delicious."

I smile at her enthusiasm, even if my stomach rolls over at the thought of anything even remotely resembling alcohol at this hour. The drinks from last night are hitting me like a ton of bricks. My throat feels dry and my head is pounding.

"Sit." I feel Phantom's hand on my back. He pulls out a kitchen chair for me, his eyes raking over the button-down I've tied in a knot at my waist. I can see his Adam's apple bob, and his eyes grow dark as he rakes them over my face.

I want to kiss him good morning, want to get close to that soft shirt that covers his hard, thick body, and wrap myself in his scent, his heat. Typical morning after a first date feelings for an anything but typical morning after a first date situation.

Our kids are setting the table, and if my nose isn't deceiving me, Daisy has made pancakes, bacon, and eggs.

"I can't remember the last time anyone cooked for me," I say, washing down two Advil with a large swallow of coffee. "Everything smells amazing. Can I help?"

Holly sets a plate loaded with pancakes in the middle of the table. "We got this," she says. Then she gives me a toothy grin. "If we cook, we get to make whatever we want." She points to the brown splotches in the pancakes. "Chocolate chips."

One look at Jax proves he's as excited about the meal as the girls, and a mixture of joy and sadness sweeps over me.

I work every Saturday and clean on Sunday, so I never see my son play with kids his age or have sleepovers. He's always over at Tera's with his best friend Ryan or at the shop with me while I clean. How many moments like this has my son shared with other families?

This feeling. It's nothing I've had since Clara and I were little. The realization hits me hard. I do okay by my son, but how much better or happier could his life be?

The food is all laid out, so the girls take their seats at the table. Phantom carries a chair from the dining room and sits at the head of the table, directly across from me.

We're both quiet as we eat, letting the kids' chatter fill the room.

"How many tattoos do you have?" Jax asks between mouthfuls of bacon.

"Loads," Phantom says.

"Do you have a favorite?" Jax asks. "One that means a lot to you?"

I rub the ring finger where a tiny heart has faded so much it's almost tough to tell what it is anymore.

I study Phantom as he nods at his daughters. "The ones I got for my girls," he says, without even hesitating. "Those mean the most to me. They all have stories. They all mean something to me, but these two mean more than anything."

Jax's eyes are wide as he looks from Holly and Daisy then back at Phantom. "What are they?"

"Can I tell him, Dad?" Daisy chugs the last of her mock-mosa and gets out of her chair.

"Mm-hm." Phantom sort of grunts, and Daisy gets out of her chair and stands next to her dad.

"Right here," Daisy says, pointing to Phantom's chest. "He has a holly leaf with berries that are heart-shaped instead of round. There's a cool daisy right next to it over his heart for me." She shrugs one shoulder. "If Dad ever has any more kids, he's going to need to name them something small because there's not a lot of room left there."

Phantom nearly spits his coffee, then swats his daughter's shoulder. "Hilarious," he says. "Maybe I'll get a dog and cover up your tattoos with a picture of his face."

"You would never." Daisy wraps her arms around her dad's neck and says, "Just wait, Dad. In three years, I can get a tattoo."

"Try five," he snaps. "You're thirteen, Dais, and I'm not consenting."

"You have them." Daisy points at her dad. "I want a full sleeve of art."

"That'd be sick," Jax says.

"I'm going to be sick," Phantom chimes in. "Before you go inking yourself with pictures of plushie toys and shit, at least be old enough to order a drink. You can order one for me while you're at it, so I don't break the fingers of whoever is stupid enough to put art on my baby."

I can just imagine Phantom losing his mind, seeing a cute little kitten on Daisy's arm or ankle.

When my fork scrapes an entirely empty plate, I look down and realize I've eaten all my pancakes and three whole slices of bacon. I choke down a little of the mock-mosa, but the acid in the orange juice reminds me that I'm still not back to normal after the drinks from last night.

"That was absolute heaven," I say. I walk to the sink with my empty plate in hand. "Thank you, girls. Now, if you'll tell me where everything goes, I'm going to do these dishes."

"Like hell you will." Phantom comes up behind me and takes the dirty plate right from my hand. He turns to Jax. "You and your mom are off duty today. Why don't you go find something to watch on television. I'll do these dishes."

Holly and Daisy squeal and race out of there so fast, my son looks from me to them with a mixture of regret and worry on his face.

"Mom, should I…"

I shake my head and smile. "Go on," I tell him. "Go with the girls."

Once we're alone, Phantom leans forward, lightly pinning me between the sink and his hips. My breath catches, and I lean back against him instinctively, my rear end pressing against the firmness behind the zipper of his jeans.

"Phantom," I murmur, "you…"

"Arouse you?" His whisper against my hair is warm and rich, his voice sending shivers of electricity through my body. "Make you want to do filthy, filthy things to me?"

I turn to face him, and he rests his hands on the edge of the sink, caging me between his hips and the counter. "That's exactly what I was thinking," I say, daring myself to meet his eyes.

"Back atcha, babe," he says, then taps the side of my butt firmly with a hand. "Now, go hang with the kids while I clean. You can damn well bet I'm going to take you up on that the first chance we get."

The next thing I feel is a strong hand against my forehead. "Poppy?"

My eyes fly open, and I see Phantom above me, looking worried.

"What is it? What happened?"

"You fell asleep on the couch," he says. He glares hard and holds the back of his hand against my forehead, then the side of my neck. "But your face is beet red. You're burning up. I think you have a fever."

"Really? I can't be sick. I'm…" But as soon as I try to sit up, it hits me.

My head is pounding like someone drove a dump truck across my forehead. My throat feels scratchy when I try to say anything, and despite my best intentions, I can't muster the energy to sit. All I can do is slump my head right back where it was against the back of the couch.

Jax's worried voice breaks through my fog. "I was just sick with the flu. I must have given it to her."

"Don't you worry, little man. I've got meds, and your mom doesn't have to work until Tuesday, right? The shop's closed today and tomorrow?"

"I can't believe you remembered that," I whisper.

"I pay attention to the shit that matters," he says. "Jax, you go play with the girls. Swim if you want. Last night, a couple of my friends packed up some things from your room and brought them over. You probably have some shorts or something you can swim in. I'm going to get your mom tucked in."

"Mom, is it okay?"

"Go ahead, honey."

I hear Jax's feet pound toward the back doors, and Phantom yells, "Girls, if you're going to kayak, get Jax a vest! Vests on if you're on the channel!"

I squint open my eyes. "Phantom, I don't want to get you and the kids sick. I'll call my mom…"

He doesn't answer but, instead, slides his hands under my knees and picks me up off the couch like I weigh nothing. He's so strong, so warm.

I let myself be carried up the stairs, but to my surprise, he doesn't take me to the guest room at the end of the hall. He turns the opposite direction, toes open a door, and puts me on top of a massive king-sized bed.

His bed.

"Wait here," he says.

I don't think I'd have the strength to move if I tried.

He's gone maybe five minutes before I feel him sit on the bed beside me. "Take this."

I look down at the bottle of maximum-strength cold and flu medicine and the large glass of water. I don't even argue. I take the cup of medicine, drink it down, and wash it back with water.

"Thank you."

"You can thank me when you're better. Now, rest. I'm going to bring you tea with honey. What else do you want?"

I feel his hand stroking my hair back from my face. I open my eyes and shake my head weakly. "I can't let you take care of me. I…"

He rests his head on my forehead, his dark-blue eyes blazing as he looks at me. "You can and you will. I'll have clothes and shit brought over from your house. You're going to stay in this bed and rest and let me take care of you and Jax until you're better. You hear me?"

"Okay," I whisper, finally giving in, closing my eyes, and sighing.

Phantom tucks me in a little tighter, and then I feel him go still. He's on the bed beside me, but he's not moving or saying anything. He sits there quietly until the room goes dark behind my eyes. His blankets are so cozy, his bed so perfect. Everything in my body hurts, but I smell him and feel his presence close to me.

Before I know it, everything goes dark.

TWELVE
PHANTOM

"JAX! COME INSIDE A SEC," I shout through the patio doors, relieved to see the kids all wearing their life vests. I'm happy to see they are not only getting along, but they're doing the right thing while they're outside on the channel.

Jax bounces across the lawn, his longish brown hair flopping over his eyes. "Hey," he says, looking worried. "Is my mom okay?"

"She's great," I assure him. "I'm going to send some guys over to check on your house and grab some things for your mom. You cool staying here until your mom's better? I'll get you to school tomorrow, so backpack, clothes, whatever you're going to want." I hold up my phone. "If they missed anything when they brought over your stuff, tell me what's missing, and I'll get it."

Jax describes his backpack and the clothes he wants. I shoot off a text to Savage and ask the prospects to give me updates on the cleanup.

"Phantom?" When I look up from my phone, Jax is

standing a few feet away. He looks like he wants to go back outside, but his feet are stuck in place.

"What's up?" I ask.

Jax doesn't say anything at first, but then he crosses the living room. "Are you my mom's boyfriend now?"

The question takes me by surprise. I don't know what to say. "Does she have another one?"

Jax shakes his head. "She's never had one. Not that I ever knew about." He's quiet again, but he's biting his lip and picking at his fingernails.

"Hey." I lower a brow at him. "You got something on your mind, I'm all ears."

Jax shrugs. "Mom is just... I don't know. She's always so tired. She doesn't seem tired around you. She seems happy."

I nod. "She's had a hard run. It's not easy raising kids, working a job. I get that. Sometimes being an adult is shit, plain and simple. But she loves you, and I think she loves what she does. A little rest here will do her good. Yeah?"

Jax nods, but then he comes up close to me. He's a skinny kid. Tall, with lightly tanned skin and the same wide brown eyes as his mom. "Thank you for taking care of her. No one ever does. She won't let me and..." He trails off. "Just thank you."

An unexpected tightness grips my chest. Sometimes I forget how much of what we're going through affects our kids. I reach out and clamp a hand on Jax's shoulder. "You're a good kid, but remember, you're a *kid*. It's not your job to take care of your mom." As I say the words, I realize this is the same song and dance I've been giving Holly and Daisy. Same issues, different parents. Somehow, the shit is more relatable than I want it to be.

I jerk a thumb, motioning for him to go back outside. "Go on," I tell him. "Before the girls kayak down the channel without you."

He nods, but before he leaves, he gives me a huge smile. Then he takes off running toward the backyard.

My next call is to my lawyer. "Hey," I tell him, knowing he's got me on caller ID. I wouldn't call on a Sunday—and he wouldn't answer—if it weren't important.

"What?" he asks, getting right to the point.

"There was a break-in last night. Nothing stolen, though."

I hear him suck air. "Your place? The compound? You make a report?"

"The woman who owns the salon. Poppy." If Shayla is behind this, her motivation could either be jealousy or revenge. I'm not taking any chances. "We were out together with our kids when it happened."

I listen as my lawyer tells me exactly what he needs.

"Got it," I say. "On it."

We end the call, and I text Savage.

> Me: Upstairs in the kid's room. Get his backpack, everything you can see that he'd need to draw, and a bunch of clothes. Bring it all.

> Savage: I'm there now. Had to bring in the girls. There's too much here for the jackass prospects to clean. Stella's in charge.

Whatever it takes.

> Me: Good call. And the other thing?

> Savage: Tiny complication. Viper handled it.

> Me: Hospital?

> Savage: The other guy. Shattered ribs and a black eye. Nothing permanent. Message sent. Next run should go smooth.

I don't reply. I hate that I can't be there myself. I gave the order for Viper to handle the shitheads trying to horn in on the deal we worked with Elliott. But it should have been me—my knuckles, my fists.

> Savage: Jizz has been dealt with.

I like the text but don't reply. It's what we do. Deal with problems. Sweep up messes. Keep our house neat because our business can get dirty.

I rub my eyes and head into the kitchen. I take out my frustration on some carrots and celery. If Poppy's going to get better, she's going to need some soup. If I expect her to stay here, she's also going to need the truth.

The room is dark and quiet. I hear the soft sounds of Poppy breathing and rustling under the covers.

"Phantom?" Her voice is weak and thin.

"Hey." I set the tray I'm carrying on my bedside table and open the drapes just a crack to let in some light. "I brought lunch."

I head over to the bed and help Poppy sit up, fluffing some pillows behind her.

"You brought me soup?" she asks quietly.

"It's the only thing I can cook," I chuckle. "The kids make pancakes and all that shit, but I've got one trick. This is it. Chicken noodle soup."

She takes a deep breath then covers her mouth and coughs. "Sorry," she rasps. "It smells amazing."

I sit on the side of the bed and put the tray on her lap. "Eat," I tell her. "Then rest. I got my brothers bringing over Jax's clothes and backpack. I asked them to update me on the cleanup and to bring whatever they could for you—clothes, hairbrush, whatever."

She sets the spoon down on the tray and shakes her head. Even sick, her deep brown eyes glassy and her cheeks flushed, she is fucking beautiful. I watch her draw her lower lip into her mouth and sigh. "You don't have to do all this," she says. "I'm going to get you sick staying here."

I shake my head. "My immune system's like a rock," I tell her. My guts churn, and I realize I'm feeling fucking nervous. Me. Nervous. I push past it because there's no other way to do this. "After you've been to prison a couple times, you're around so much shit, you toughen up pretty quick."

I meet her eyes.

"At least, I did."

She considers what I said, but she doesn't flinch. Doesn't look horrified. "Can I ask what happened?"

I lace my fingers together and crack my knuckles. "When I was younger, I didn't have the same discretion I've got now. A couple of fights got out of hand. Assault, public intoxication. Stupid shit when I was careless."

She sips the tea I brought her. "Why are you telling me this?"

"Not exactly first-date information. But you're in my house, in my bed. You should know what there is to know." I know being honest with her could drive her away. Make a woman like this get up and run for the hills. Her ma's in local government, for fuck's sake. I don't know how much Mama's going to like her baby dating an ex-con.

"Is there more I should know?" she asks, her voice raspy. "Because I've seen a lot, and I have a few opinions of my own. But if there's more you want to share..."

I shake my head. "You got the highlights."

She takes another spoonful of soup. "My God, Phantom. This is good, and it's not just because I'm sick." She leans back against the pillows and sighs. "I'm glad you told me. There's something I think you should know."

I brace for whatever's coming. I can take it. I've been

insulted. Called a criminal or worse. Called worthless by the people who were supposed to love me. Fuck, Shayla's favorite nickname for me is loser. Whatever Poppy thinks, it can't be anything I haven't heard before. So why am I tensing up like I'm bracing for a punch that I know is going to hurt?

"Lay it on me," I say.

Her eyes are closed, but there's a smile on her lips. "You're gorgeous," she says. "And funny. You've been gentle with me and nothing but perfect with my son. Your daughters adore you, and I haven't seen you do anything but the right thing since I met you."

"Go back to the first thing." I scoot closer and put my hand on her knee. Even though the blankets separate my skin from hers, I need to touch her right now. Need to feel her close to me. "Gorgeous. More about that."

"Mmmmm,'" she moans and laughs softly, which is quickly followed up by a wicked cough. "Sorry," she croaks.

I smooth the hair back from her face and pour out another dose of flu meds. "Drink this so you can go back to telling me how sexy you think I am."

"I didn't say sexy, but…" She swallows the meds and washes them down with water. "God, you are. If I weren't sick right now…"

I move close and rest the back of my wrist against her forehead. "You're not burning up again, so you're not delirious. You know what you're saying. I'm going to want you to finish that sentence."

"I will," she murmurs and then drifts back into sleep.

Poppy sleeps through Sunday afternoon. Daisy makes dinner for us, and I try to bring Poppy a burger, but she's snoring and looks too peaceful to wake.

Savage brought over a bunch of things from Poppy's house, and Holly spent the afternoon washing Jax's school clothes along with the girls'. Turns out that Jax's elementary school is right across the street from Daisy's junior high. Dropping everybody off in the morning will be no big deal.

After dinner, I do the dishes while Holly crams for a math exam in her room, and Jax and Daisy work on a comic book at the kitchen table.

I'm sitting on the patio staring off at the blue water of the channel when my phone rings. I set my beer down and swipe the touchscreen.

"What?" I ask.

Savage is on the other line. "We got something."

I listen as he fills me in. It's a rumor, but if we can confirm what he's saying is true, I might just have the evidence I need to prove Shayla was behind the break-in at Poppy's.

"Get me a name," I bark.

"Phantom." Savage says it quietly, but there's no mistaking the warning in his voice.

"Get me the fucking name," I tell him.

I disconnect the call and drain my beer, then stalk inside.

Jax and Daisy look up as I enter. "Dad, can we have some ice cream?" Daisy asks.

"Yeah," I grumble, yanking open the fridge and grabbing another beer. Then it hits me. "Wait, you had dessert after dinner."

Daisy shrugs one shoulder. "You looked distracted. It was worth a try."

"You little shit." I put the beer back in the fridge without opening it. "I'm never so distracted I won't notice a second dessert." I come around to the kitchen table and mess up Daisy's hair.

"Dad!" she squeals, and I drop down into a seat next to her.

"What's this?" I ask, pointing.

"Jax is a super-good artist," she says, pointing to the paper.

"Yeah?" I tug the sketchbook that Savage brought along with a bunch of other shit from the house earlier today close so I can get a good look. "Shit, kid." I scan the panels of pencil drawings. "This is fucking impressive."

"Dad." Daisy shakes her head. "You swear too much."

I snort but take note. "This is *super* impressive," I say, echoing what Daisy said a minute ago. "This is good, kid. You got what it takes."

"You think so?" Jax's eyes light up at my compliment. "You think I'm good enough to be a tattoo artist?"

I flex my left arm so my bicep swells. I hold his sketchbook up beside the inside of my arm. "Your shit?" I lift a brow at Daisy. "Your *stuff* is way better than half the *stuff* I have inked on my body. Look at this."

I don't tell Jax how many of my tatts were inked in prison or at parties in the compound by guys who had more balls than talent.

Jax's grin is so big, I can't help smiling. "I'll be your first client, kid. Got plenty of skin left to cover."

"For real?"

"I'll be your second client," Daisy says, taking the notepad back from me.

Getting the kids to bed is a piece of cake. Jax heads to the guest room, and Holly offers to wake him up since he doesn't have an alarm clock in the room. I kiss my girls goodnight, then knock on the door of the guest room.

"Hi," Jax says.

I nod at him. "You got what you need, little man? You need lunch money, anything like that?"

He laughs. "No. That's all settled at school. I'll just have some juice or something in the morning before we leave."

I scan the room and notice Jax's art is spread out over the made bed and his clothes are in piles on the floor, but the piles look pretty organized.

"You're a great kid," I tell him.

He looks at me, a funny expression on his face. "Thanks," he says.

I ruffle his hair and say goodnight. Then I head to

my bedroom. I quietly walk into the bathroom and brush my teeth, then I climb on top of the bed beside Poppy. I check her temp, but she feels cooler. She groans and rolls over onto her side, scooting her ass toward me. I have to physically restrain myself from rolling over and sliding a hand along the curves of her thighs, up her ass, and fisting the long, tangled waves of her hair.

I lie flat on my back, pull a pillow over my head, and count backward from a million.

The next morning, I jump in the shower and dress without waking Poppy. I hope all this sleep helps her turn a corner. Not that I'm anxious for her to be healthy enough to leave. In fact, I'm shocked how comfortable I am with her here. With Jax at the kitchen table beside my girls.

I could get used to this.

Taking care of someone. Looking out for her. But this is a new start for me. I've got the girls. I'm staying at the house, not in my shitty bunk at the compound.

I could *definitely* get used to this.

"Five-minute warning," I say, pointing at the door. "Shoes on. Get your backpacks. You know what to do."

Jax immediately clears his plate from the table, and I throw some berries and melon onto a plate, grab a couple slices of toast from the stack Daisy made for the kids, and pour a huge glass of orange juice.

"Knock, knock," I say, nudging open my bedroom door.

Poppy's eyes flutter open, and she looks at the plate

in my hands. "I thought you said you couldn't cook." She smiles, and her color actually looks good.

I feel her forehead, and unless I'm totally wrong, she's broken the fever. I set the plate on the tray and put the juice on the bedside table.

"I put this shit on a plate. I didn't make it." I lean down and kiss the top of her head before I realize what I'm doing. "Shit, ah... Toast. Daisy. Daisy made it. I've got to go. Taking the kids to school." I turn to leave before I realize I didn't ask how she's feeling. "You okay? I'll be back after drop-off."

She nods. "Sweaty and gross, but I think I'm better."

"Rest." I point a finger at her, then close the bedroom door behind me.

I'm dashing down the stairs when my phone buzzes with a text.

> **Law Man:** Good news. Emergency hearing date set. Family court tomorrow at nine.

This is good news, but it's all happening faster than I expected. I wonder if the break-in at Poppy's had anything to do with the date being set so fast.

> **Me:** Will Shayla be there?

"Dad! We got to go!"

I slide into my boots and put my phone in my pocket. I can find out the details later. As much as I want custody of my kids, as much as I want Shayla out of their lives, once the court date is set, the shit's really going to hit the fucking fan. And I plan on making sure no one I care about gets caught in Shayla's crossfire.

THIRTEEN
POPPY

I DON'T EVEN KNOW how much time has passed. When I wake up, it's dark in Phantom's bedroom, and I feel like I've lost all sense of what day it is.

On the one hand, I feel like I've been here forever, and that's not a bad thing. But on the other hand, I've been wearing the same T-shirt and boxers for however long it's been, and I'm anxious to get back to normal.

Shit, the salon.

I grab my phone from the bedside table, thankful that Phantom has kept it charged.

> Me: Please tell me this flu doesn't last more than a day or two.

She replies in seconds.

> Clara: Is that why I haven't heard from you? I was hoping after your family date you'd been locked away in a sex dungeon with that fine-as-eff man, but since you didn't ask me to watch Jax, I assumed you were blowing me off.

I sometimes do blow off my sister's texts, if I'm honest. I love her to pieces, but I see her Tuesday through Saturday at the salon. If she blows up my phone Sunday or Monday, it's usually to bitch about Mom. I stopped trying to change our mother years ago. Clara, the youngest and the more stubborn of the two of us, has not.

> Me: Well, you're not completely wrong. I've been at his place with Jax, but not for the reasons you think.

I include a sick emoji and hit send. I feel like every inch of my body has been soaked in sweat, then dried, and soaked again. Utterly disgusting.

I head into the bathroom and grab a towel from the small closet next to the shower. I'm shocked to find my makeup bag and a plastic bag filled with toiletries that someone must have brought from my house.

I can't believe how out of it I've been. And he's just stepped in and thought of everything. I can't remember a time when I wasn't responsible for everyone and everything. As sick as I've been, I swear just having time to sleep has got me feeling better already.

I turn on the water and check the notification from my sister, then strip down while the water heats up.

Just having those sweaty clothes off my body feels so much better. I'm going to have to strip Phantom's bed and disinfect everything in his room.

> Clara: So, tell me you're going to fuck him once you're better, Pop?

When I don't respond right away, three more texts come in rapid succession.

> Clara: Tell me you already did and then you got sick.

> Clara: Tell me something.

> Clara: Details!!

I hesitate before texting back.

Me: No, I have not and...it's complicated.

And... That's the problem. God knows I want him. He's beautiful and thoughtful. But I hardly know him. We've both got kids to care for, and he's got Shayla to deal with it. It's all so darned complicated.

> Clara: What's complicated? Make it simple, sis, and hit that. Come on!

I ignore her text and check the water. It's perfect. I don't have my expensive salon shampoo, but there is some drugstore product that Phantom must have bought to replace the stuff that was ruined in the break-in.

That man has thought of absolutely everything.

Based on the label and the berry scent, it's the same stuff he buys the girls. Something about that fills my heart to almost bursting. I shove the feelings away and focus on what I started texting Clara about in the first place.

> Me: Can you cover the salon tomorrow? I'll call my clients tonight and reschedule as many as I can, but I need to get home and sort some things out and be sure I'm over this before I come back to work.

> Clara: You fuck him, I'll cover you.

A text like that doesn't deserve a reply. Even if it's a deal I'd gladly agree to.

The water feels absolutely glorious—hot and clean. Just what I need. I scrub myself every place possible—twice—and wish I had a razor so I could shave my legs. I didn't think to check the bag, but when I bend over to touch my stubble, I feel a little light-headed… So maybe the shaving can wait. Once my hair is clean and I feel almost like me again, I wrap myself in a towel, blot my hair dry, and climb out of the shower.

I pad into Phantom's room and look around to see if I have anything to wear when the door swings open.

"Poppy? You up? I—"

Phantom takes one look at me, my hands clutching one of his towels over my chest.

"I, uh…" he says.

We both freeze and laugh. I point back toward the bathroom. "I found my toiletries. Thank you."

He's staring at me like a lion sizing up a tasty-looking gazelle.

"Phantom?" I say, clutching the towel a little tighter. "Are you okay?"

He shakes his head and nods. "Sorry. Fuck me." He's beside me in a second, his hand on my arm. "Why are you out of bed?"

"Drenched with sweat," I say, lifting a lock of my hair. "But the good news is, I think the fever broke."

His eyes go wide and his nostrils flare.

"Phantom, I'm kidding." I smile at him, despite the fact that I think my hair might be starting to drip on his bedroom floor. "I took a shower. I'm getting better. I felt disgusting and wanted to clean up."

"Poppy." He swallows hard and drags a hand through his beard. "Clothes."

He points to me, and I follow his finger, looking confused. I'm giving this man the view of a lifetime of my cleavage.

Oh. My. God.

I freeze, not sure whether to tug the towel up and risk exposing my other bits or let go of the towel and adjust it, which would give him a whole eyeful of literally everything.

I might as well just dance naked across the bedroom at this point. I start to back into the bathroom. "Um, I'll just find something later?"

"Poppy. Wait."

I stop, my bare toes squeaking on the smooth wood floor. I look at Phantom, my fingers locked in a battle between the towel and the forces of gravity that seem to really want me to give this man a show.

Something unspoken but powerful pulses between us, and heat floods my body. His lips are parted, and he reaches to move a wet lock of my hair from my face. We don't say anything. All I hear is the pounding of my heart and the soft breaths as he flares his nostrils and sucks in a deep breath.

"You're fucking stunning." I don't know when he moved closer, but I have to look up now to meet his eyes.

I stare into his face, and my fingers, shady little bitches that they are, loosen their hold on the towel. It slips an inch, then two, and I draw in an unsteady breath when the cool air hits my nipples.

"I want to taste you." His words are a raspy plea. "Poppy, you make me... You..."

Holding the towel loosely with one hand—because why bother fighting, gravity's going to win this one— my eyes flutter closed. "Do it," I tell him. "Phantom, please, do it..."

He drops to his knees on the hard floor and lifts his hands to cup both of my breasts. I suck in a breath as torrents of heat flow through my body. His thumbs stroke my erect nipples, his rough skin scraping the tender flesh and practically bringing me to my knees.

"Dad?"

The sound of Daisy's voice outside the door breaks the moment. Phantom is on his feet with lightning speed and lifting the edge of the towel to cover my breasts. "Bathroom," he says quietly. "I'll go see what's up. Your clothes are there."

He points to a small suitcase that I'm going to guess belongs to one of the girls. It's teal blue and covered in faded stickers.

"Thank you," I pant, which somehow feels like the wrong thing to say. Then I turn, run into the bathroom, and close the door behind me.

My nipples are aching, and a flood of wetness has pooled between my legs. I need to cover up, get dressed, and lock my sex drive back down. This man is getting under my skin. And now that I've had a touch, a taste, I want so much more. I've never felt more terrified.

I'm feeling well enough to join the family at dinner. After the kids have eaten, I send them off to do homework, while Phantom and I stay behind to do the dishes.

"I have to be at family court tomorrow." He says the words quietly. "Do you think you'd be willing to go with me?"

I almost drop a glass as I'm trying to load it into the dishwasher. "Go with you? You mean, as a witness? Will I have to testify?"

"No, that's not what I meant." He plants his hands on the sink and stares at the stack of dishes. "I thought it would be safer for you. Just in case...Shayla, you know."

I don't know. "What do you mean safer?" I set the glass on the rack and come up behind him. I put a hand on his back. "Do you think she's behind what happened at my house, Phantom? Why would you be worried about my safety?"

He sighs. "She might be. I don't know for sure, but she was served notice of the emergency hearing. It'll go forward whether she shows or not, but I'd feel better if I know the kids are safe in school. And I want you safe. I want you with me so I know you are."

I step close to him and rest my cheek against his back. It's an instinct I give in to but immediately regret. I pull back and step away, not sure what to say. I hurry to get back to loading dishes.

I have never felt more cared for, more protected by anyone in my entire life. Not even when I was with Michael. I feel like a traitor even admitting it. But this man, this tattooed ex-convict, biker, father, mystery of a man, has already been more of a hero in my story than anyone ever has.

"Poppy?" He tosses a sponge into the sink and turns to face me. His arms are crossed over his chest, and he waits, those denim-blue eyes insistent.

"What time is the hearing?" I ask.

"Nine. I figured I'd drop all the kids at school and then head to the courthouse."

Clara is going to cover the salon tomorrow, so I can take the day to do whatever. Sleep, clean my house. I know Phantom said he had people doing it, but I can't imagine anyone will take better care of my house than I will. I think back to the broken glass, the trashed papers, the overturned furniture.

"Do you really think Shayla's behind what happened at my house?" I ask.

He turns to the fridge and grabs a beer. "You want one?" he asks. "Or you think you'll want some cold medicine tonight?"

Right now, the thought of an ice-cold beer sounds like bliss. "I'd love one."

He opens the bottles, and we sit back down at the table, the dishes only half done.

"I put the word out, and we got some names. I don't have proof yet, but I'm close."

"Why?" I ask, taking a long sip of the beer. It bubbles and fizzes on my tongue. Cold and refreshing after so many hours hot from my fever. "What could she possibly have against me?"

Phantom rolls his neck. "Shayla isn't herself. I don't know what's gotten into her. The shit with the kids and the salon... That's not the half of it. She could be pissed I paid your bill, she could be pissed we went to dinner with the kids. Could be nothing, could be anything."

All of a sudden, the beer sits heavy on my stomach. "How would she know?" I ask. "How would she know we went out together? Is she still hung up on you?"

Phantom shakes his head and barks out a bitter laugh. He reaches across the table and takes my hand just like he did in the restaurant. He laces his fingers through mine, and despite the worry and fear, I feel calmer.

"Babe, I don't know. I don't know if she has any idea

we were out. The last time I saw Shayla, which was the day after I met you, she was standing in the driveway of the compound, calling me a loser and threatening to call the cops on me for taking the kids." He strokes the back of my hand with a thumb. "It's all legal and above board. I'm entitled to have them whenever they want to be with me. And if the court agrees with me, I'll have them permanently."

"Is she dangerous?"

"Babe, I've known Shayla since junior high. We met when we were Daisy's age. She was my first everything. First fuck, first kiss. She got knocked up when we were seventeen and stood by me through all the stupid shit I did. But things change. People change. I think I've changed for the better in some ways, but don't get me wrong, I'm an asshole through and through. Shayla didn't start out the way she is now, but the change happened quick."

I wrap my hands around his and squeeze. His hands are scarred and rough, but somehow, they fit me.

"Do you think she'd hurt me or Jax?" I ask, suddenly wondering what might have happened if we'd been home when the break-in happened, but I can't go there.

"That's a chance I don't want to take." His eyes bore into mine. "I want to protect you both. And right now, I can only do that if you're with me."

He leans over the table, and I lean in too, until our noses practically touch over our clasped hands. "Stay with me, Poppy. Stay here for as long as it takes to sort this out."

I close my eyes and lower my head until our foreheads touch. I can't agree to it. Stay here? What am I going to do, move my son in to the home of a man I've known for one week?

But when I open my eyes, I refuse to believe that the man who made me soup, who fed me medicine, whose daughters are kind, gentle, wonderful young women could have a dark side so bleak I can't handle it.

There's been no one in my life since Michael. No one I wanted. No one I could even picture being with me past a single date. Technically, Phantom and I are still on our first date.

"Will you take me to my place?" I ask. "After the court appearance."

He nods. "Whatever you want."

I draw in a shaky breath and lower my lips to kiss his knuckles. "Okay. I'll go to court with you."

That's all I can promise him for now. I can't give him any more of me. After tomorrow, I have to go back to work. I have to get back to my life, whatever that looks like now.

But how am I ever going to let go of something I want so badly?

FOURTEEN
PHANTOM

HOLLY LOANS POPPY a sweater to wear over the dress she wore on our first date. We don't have time to get nice clothes for her to wear to court, but with the sweater covering up the one bare shoulder, she looks fucking sexy and a hell of a lot better than the rest of the jokers lined up in the halls of family court. I'm wearing dress pants and a dress shirt without a tie, and I'm sweating because I'm so nervous.

I've got my fingers laced through Poppy's, and we're sitting side by side on a shitty wooden bench that reminds me of going to church. Your ass never forgets a church pew, and this feels as uncomfortable as it did when I was seven. That was probably the last time I set foot in a house of worship. With seats like this, it's no wonder why.

"Owen." My lawyer extends his hand to me. "Good to see you."

I shoot a look at Poppy, whose lips curl into a small smile at hearing my given name.

"Thanks for handling this, Ed." I motion toward Poppy. "This is Poppy Vallejo. Poppy, my lawyer, Ed."

Poppy and Ed shake hands, and Ed gets rights down to business. "I've also filed a temporary restraining order that applies to you, Poppy, and both girls. I expect the judge to rule on that today as well."

Poppy squeezes my hand, and I don't even need to look at her to know what she's thinking. "Poppy has a son," I remind Ed. "Is his name on those papers?"

Ed curses under his breath. "How old?"

"Ten," Poppy supplies.

"I'll talk to the clerk. Let them know, under the circumstances with the break-in, it's a detail I overlooked. We'll get it amended."

Ed looks us over and locks on us holding hands. "Is this something I need to know about?" he asks. "If you're dating the woman who gave a sworn declaration to the court, that could call her impartiality into question."

Poppy releases my hand. "I was just trying to be supportive," she explains. "This is stressful. Probably as much for me as for him."

Ed nods. "Shayla's been served with a notice to appear, but she doesn't have to. I talked to her lawyer last night, and I don't think she's going to show. We both think there's almost no chance the judge won't rule in your favor, but…" He glares at me. "Just remember. Nothing's guaranteed in family court. Taking the girls away from their mother completely is only going to be granted on a temporary basis. Just stay quiet, let me do the talking, and no matter what happens, keep your cool."

He gives me this talk every time.

"Got it." I move to take Poppy's hand but then remember what Ed said. I shoot her a look.

The court clerk calls my last name, and Ed motions for us to go into the courtroom.

"That's us," I say, nodding at Poppy. I stroke my beard nervously, and she gives me a look. I'm starting to understand Poppy's many expressions. The way she blinks and works her lips like she's whispering to herself when she's thinking. The way she stares at her son like he's water and she's dying of thirst. And the way she looks at me. Like she is drawn in and yet repelled—or maybe is just pulling back—at the same time.

I get it.

There hasn't been a woman I've wanted to make mine for more than a night since Shayla. I told Poppy I wanted her with me so I could protect her, and that's true, but the minute Ed's back is turned, I lace my fingers through hers and squeeze.

Maybe this isn't just about her body, her kindness, the tiredness around her eyes that make me want to burn down the world so she can get some rest.

Just as with the ink on my chest, I haven't believed that I have room in, around, or anywhere near my heart for anyone but my daughters.

I'm an asshole through and through. And I've been wrong before. Maybe I've been wrong about how big that space around my heart really is.

"That was fast," Poppy murmurs against my ear as we stand and wait for the judge to dismiss us.

It was fast and easy. Too easy, really. I shake my lawyer's hand, and he tells me I don't have to wait.

Once the court stamps everything and does whatever they do, he'll have all the paperwork confirming that I've been granted not only full temporary custody of the girls, but a restraining order against Shayla that keeps her away from me and the kids except for scheduled visits through a social worker. That's going to be a lotta bullshit, appointments and scheduling, but I'll do it if it means I get to keep the kids with me.

"You still want to go to your place?" I ask once we're back in my truck. As if it has a mind of its own, my right hand reaches out to hold hers.

"Yeah," she says quietly.

There's something in her voice I don't like. "Was that too much for you?" After everything I've been through, I still fucking hate being in a courthouse. Seeing the bailiffs and judges brings back too many painful memories. I just try to remind myself that as long as there's nothing they can put cuffs on me for, I'm all right.

I realize now that, having Poppy with me, I was way less fucked in the head than I normally am about judges and legal shit. But she probably hasn't been through anything like this before. She hasn't even gone through a divorce.

"No," she says quietly. "Maybe. I don't know. It just broke my heart for your girls. Having the court decide when and how they can see their mom. I know it's what's best for them, but it's hard not to wonder what would have happened if Michael hadn't passed away."

She stares straight ahead through the windshield as she talks. "I don't want to disrespect his memory. He was a good guy. My high school sweetheart. But you talked about people changing. Michael was changing. He changed, I guess. I mean, after Jax was born."

I listen until we pull into the driveway outside her house. There's a bike parked halfway down the block that I recognize as one of the prospect's.

Good. I told them surveillance.

I kill the engine and turn to face Poppy. "What do you mean changed?"

She shakes her head, those long brown waves moving around her face. "I don't know. I think my mom knows something about it, but to be honest, I don't want to know. If he was cheating, what does it matter now? All it would do is change the memories I have. Can you imagine not being able to confront him? Knowing a secret and having to live with it like that? Sometimes I wonder if I'm so damned tired all the time because all I ever do is work on keeping all the questions and all the suspicions buried." She licks her lips. "But they are fighting to get out. I need to know the truth, don't I? What kind of person would I be if I said I really don't want to know?"

"The kind of person who's protecting her peace.

Fuck, Poppy. Your dad died after he built your salon. You were a widow with a two-year-old. Do you really think knowing any more about how your husband died or what he was up to before he passed would change your life for the better?"

She turns in the seat and faces me. "I locked up my heart when he died. I don't know if I know how to let anyone else in."

What she's saying hits me as hard as what she's not saying. She wants to let me in. And she might never be able to.

"After you've been locked up," I tell her, "it's like the only thing that matters is freedom. But you get out of a cell, and you're right back in another kind of prison. The kind of prison people put you in. Bills and bosses. People's opinions of you. Prejudice." I shake my head. "Any door I've ever opened, I had to break my way through. A little lock ain't going to keep me out of where I want to go. You just got to let me know it's okay, and I'll break down the fucking door if I have to."

I jerk a thumb toward her house. "Not like that. I don't fucking go where I'm not wanted. But if I am…"

Her lips part and her breathing goes shallow.

There's a sudden rap at the window, and I turn a murderous gaze to the prospect who should be watching the house, not me.

I throw open the door and slam it behind me, leaving Poppy in the truck. "What?"

The kid holds up his phone and shakes it wildly. "I'm sorry, Phantom. I'm sorry. Savage and Viper have been blowing up my phone. They said they can't reach you and it's urgent."

I curse under my breath and grab my phone. Fuck. Fuck! I turned it off while we were in court and didn't even think to turn it back on. Once I power it up, I see fifteen messages.

> Savage: Problem. Call me.

> Viper: We definitely have a problem.

> Savage: Call me the second you get this.

> Viper: Phantom, fuck. Where TF are you?

I don't bother reading the rest of them since they all say the same things. I punch in Savage's number and dial it.

"What the fuck is going on?" I bark. Poppy is still in my truck, and I want her where I can see her. Even more important, I want her safe.

Savage gets right to it. "Dylan," he says. "He was jumped. Beat bad. He's here, but you're going to want to see this. How soon can you get here."

"I need two hours, tops. He need a doctor?"

Savage grunts. "He won't go. He's conscious, but he's fucked up. He won't say what happened."

I'll get Dylan to talk. The only reason he's not talking now is he either can't because too many teeth are broken, or he fucked up and he's stalling to figure out how to spin it. I'm banking on that last thing.

"Don't let him out of your sight. Two hours." I hang up, then clap the prospect on the shoulder. "Good work. I'm going to bring her inside. Eyes on the house while we're in there."

He nods, looking relieved that I complimented him instead of tore him a new asshole for pounding on my window. I go around to the passenger side and try to remember what the fuck we were talking about.

"I'm sorry," I tell her. "Work shit. I'm going to have to go in."

She nods. "Do you need to go now? You can leave me here, and—"

I take her hand and help her climb down onto the sidewalk. I pull her hips to mine and then cup her cheeks. "Poppy. I'm not leaving you here. I'm not leaving you, period. You hear me? You may be used to people leaving or never even showing up for you. We're in this together. Come on."

I take her hand and hold it as we walk inside the house. Once we're inside, she gasps.

"It's empty," she says. "What happened?"

I motion to the place where the couch was. "The furniture that was slashed and cut is at the dump. We took pictures of everything that first night, but I had the guys take more pics so you can send them to your insurance. I'm sorry. We couldn't save a lot of your stuff."

I can only imagine how this feels to her. I show her the box where all the papers were carefully placed and follow her into the kitchen.

She opens every cabinet, pulls open the drawers in the fridge. "It's like we never lived here. This looks like a house that's up for sale. No food, no mess." She turns to me, a bewildered look on her beautiful features. "Your bikers did this? This is better than a professional cleaning crew could do if they had a week."

"There are a few women who hang around the club. They helped," I tell her.

I don't know what to say right now. She looks stunned and sad.

"Poppy, are you okay?"

"I want to meet them," she says. "I need to thank the people who did this. How many women are there? I'm going to do their hair for free for months."

I take her in my arms and hold her close. "Stop. You don't have to kiss ass or apologize. These people did it because I asked them to. We're a family, and if you're with me, you're part of it."

"Am I with you?" she asks, looking up into my face.

"Do you want to be?"

She doesn't hesitate. "Yes, but I still want to meet them."

I chuckle. "You're in luck. Stella's birthday is this weekend. We're having a party at the compound Saturday night. The girls can watch Jax, and we'll stop in. Make an appearance. You can thank them yourself, but that's it. You don't owe anybody shit, Poppy. You hear me?"

She doesn't respond. Just takes my hand and heads toward the door. "Can we go back to your place now? This doesn't even feel like home."

I do exactly what my woman asks.

———————

Poppy is quiet on the drive to my place, but she doesn't let go of my hand. "I should call my mom," she says. "Let her know what's going on."

I nod. "You want to invite her over? She might feel better if she sees where you and Jax are staying."

"Then I'll have to explain how I know you. Why we're with you. How long we're staying."

I squeeze her fingers. "You want me to talk to Mama Lori? Let her know exactly what the deal is?"

Poppy laughs. "I don't know that what you'd tell her is any better than what I'd tell her."

"I don't know," I say. "Once they get past my tattoos, my bike, and my past, moms love me."

"My mom would love you," she says. When I pull into the driveway and click the garage door open, she continues. "Mom never wanted me to marry Michael. She said there was no way I could know what was out there if I married the first man I let under my skirt." She rolls her eyes. "It's been a while, but yeah, she actually said that."

I narrow my eyes and look at the dress that sits just covering Poppy's thighs. "I love the idea of getting under your skirt."

Poppy opens the door, shaking her head. I've got to get to the club, but first, I'm going to walk her in and make sure she gets settled. I disarm the alarm and we head inside.

"Do you want me to pick the kids up from school? I'm better now, Phantom, and my car is here. I can pick up all the kids while you run to work."

I shake my head. "Get your fine ass upstairs and in bed. You have one more afternoon to rest. I'll hit the compound, take care of business, and get the kids on my way back here. Family dinner at six."

When I say family dinner, she turns and looks at me. "I'd love that. I'm going to go get changed."

She heads upstairs, and I follow her so I can change out of the dress clothes I wore to court. We walk into my bedroom together like it's something we've done every day. Like it's normal. Like it's ours. Not mine. Not my house. *Ours*.

As soon as we're inside the bedroom, she must be feeling what I am because she turns to me and just looks at me. Her eyes shimmer with tears, but she looks happy. "Phantom." She says my name and steps close to me, pressing my back against the closed bedroom door. "I don't know how to—"

My mouth is on hers before she even gets the words out. I circle her face with my hands and kiss her soft and slow. Our first real kiss. She whimpers as our tongues tangle gently, then rough, and my cock goes hard as a lead pipe.

She leans her hips against mine, and her hands are suddenly everywhere. Tugging at my hips, scratching the back of my neck. I plunge my tongue into her mouth and taste every sweet flavor that is her. But it's not enough. I need more. I want her more than I want to breathe my next breath.

I pick her up, and she wraps her legs around my hips. I stagger over to the bed and set her on her back, then graze my hand over the front of her dress.

"Poppy," I grit out, hoarse with need. "I want to—"

I don't even get the words out when she moves her hands to the top of her dress. She wriggles her arms and shoves the soft fabric down, exposing her breasts to me.

"Fuck, you're perfect."

With her lying back on my bed, her hair spilling out on the blankets, I'm speechless. I can't fucking form a coherent thought. I can't move. I forget all about time, the compound. Everything. Everything but her.

"Phantom, please..." She's breathing softly through parted lips, and she cups her tits with her hands. "I need to feel your mouth on me."

She doesn't have to ask me twice. I drop my mouth to her perfect breast and draw the entire nipple into my mouth. Her peak is hard and soft and so, so tender. She squirms and huffs hot little whimpers as I suck her nipple and squeeze her breast in my hand.

My cock is throbbing and desperate for release, but I'm in a frenzy. I want this woman worse than I've ever wanted anything. She's like a virus that has infected me, claiming me from the inside.

I lightly pinch her nipples with my fingertips until she's gasping and bucking her hips against me. But I'm not going to let the first time she comes be from dry humping me. I move my hands from her tits to her thighs, kneading and stroking her thick muscles until my hands are under her skirt.

I brush my fingers across the front of her panties,

and she's drenched. So wet that my dick jerks behind my zipper as I shove the panties to one side. I'm just about to stroke her, to touch her, when she stops me.

"Phantom. Wait."

I'm breathing hard. My cock is hard. And my self-control is difficult to pull back. But at the smallest sign from her, I freeze, my fingers under the elastic of her panties.

"This is a lot for me. I need to slow down." She rolls off the bed, adjusts her dress, and lowers her skirt to mid-thigh. She walks over to the window and stares out over the lawn.

"Did I do something wrong? Was I too rough, too…" I'm behind her in an instant, ready to apologize, ready to say or do anything to make it right if I went too far, asked for too much.

"No. God, no." She turns and faces me, her cheeks flushed as bright as when she had her fever. "You're perfect. Too perfect. If we didn't stop, I don't think I could have."

"We're consenting adults, babe," I remind her. "We can fuck when and how we want to. And if you don't want to, we wait."

She lowers her forehead against my chest and draws in a shaky breath. "I haven't felt like that with anyone, not even my husband. And if I ever felt anything even close, I definitely don't remember now."

I hold her tight against me, a selfish grin on my face. "Baby, that was not even foreplay. That was barely getting started."

She groans, and the sound travels straight to my

cock. "Soon, okay? I just need a little more time to be ready and maybe a chance to shave?"

I release her and cup her chin with my hand. "Babe, you could be hairier than a woolly fucking mammoth, and I'd still want to fuck you into our next lifetime. You hear me? You're perfect." And she is. Absolutely fucking perfect.

She sighs and looks out over my yard, so I stand behind her, wrap my arms around her, and press my still-hard cock against her ass. "When you're ready," I start, but as soon as I look out the window, the words die on my lips.

"What is it?" she asks, turning toward me. "Phantom?"

"Stay here," I tell her. I rush to my dresser, open the middle top drawer, and grab the Glock I keep there. "I saw something in the pool house. Stay here and lock the bedroom door when I leave."

I take off running down the stairs, flying through the house, and shoving past the patio doors. The pool house has cameras on it and an alarm that the kids can disable when they swim so every movement doesn't give off an alert. There's no sign of a break-in, but I swear I see something floating in the pool.

I pull on the door to the pool house, and it opens without a code. It's unlocked and unarmed. Anyone could have gotten in and done anything. They wouldn't have been able to get into the house, but still.

My weapon cocked, safety off, I look through the pool house. There's nowhere to hide but the mechanical closet, so I kick the door open to make sure it's empty. It is. No sign of anyone in here.

Certain that I'm alone, I click the safety on my gun and walk up to the edge of the pool. And then what I spotted from my bedroom comes into focus. Rats. Dead rats. At least a dozen of them. Floating in my fucking pool.

THE REST of the week flies by. Phantom must make up an excuse so he can keep the kids out while he has the pool emptied and disinfected. He doesn't talk much about what happened, and that's okay with me. We both assume it was another Shayla special. Phantom took pictures, sent them to his attorney, and that was the last we discussed it.

Between my going back to work and adjusting to a new schedule at Phantom's, I hardly have time to worry about the rats or Shayla. I've started taking the kids to school in the morning, and Phantom picks them up in the afternoon. While the social workers try to schedule meetings with Shayla to sort out when and how she can visit the girls, we just sort of hunker down in a new normal.

But there is nothing normal at all about living with a man I've only known a couple of weeks. After I freaked out on him the day we made out and found the rats, Phantom has been careful and gentle. We've slowed things way down. I don't sleep in his bed anymore, and to be honest, I miss it. Now, I sleep in the other twin bed in the room with Jax, and it's been torture.

By Saturday afternoon, I think the strain of the new situation is getting to all of us. When I come back from the salon, the girls are irritable and are snapping at each other. The pool is off-limits until at least Tuesday. Jax is unusually quiet, and it seems like the newness of our situation here is wearing off. He spends a lot of time alone in the guest room drawing, hard at work at something he hasn't wanted to share.

Phantom has to do some work, and tonight is the birthday party at the compound. I'd like to get Stella, the girl who led the cleanup efforts at my house, something nice, so I propose we all get out of the house.

"I'm going to make a quick run to the mall to pick up something to wear tonight and to buy a little gift for Stella. Anyone feel like coming along?"

Holly and Daisy look like they just won the lotto, but Jax looks miserable.

"Do I have to?" he asks. "I don't really feel like shopping."

Daisy nudges him with her elbow. "Come on. We can get smoothies." She looks to her dad. "I mean, can we get smoothies, Dad?"

Phantom grunts but is texting furiously on his phone.

I give her a grin. "I like smoothies."

"Mom, can I just stay here? I'll just stay in my room, I promise—"

I'm fixated on the fact that Jax said my room...*my*

room...like it's his. Like this is the place we belong. I don't even notice when Phantom drops his phone on the counter.

"He can come with me." He shoots me a look. "Plans for the day have changed. Gotta stop at the compound for a meeting. Jax will be perfectly safe with me. He can draw, watch TV, whatever he wants."

Jax literally looks like I just told him he could eat nothing but ice cream and pizza for the rest of his life and, instead of chores, he'll be paid to play video games until he turns eighteen. He looks elated and immediately starts begging.

"Mom, can I go with Phantom? Please!" he pleads.

I shoot Phantom a look, and just like we've known each other for months or years, not days, he motions for Jax to sit.

"Let me talk to your mother," he says, clamping a hand on Jax's shoulder. "If she says yes, we're good to go. If she says no, I'm taking my invitation back and I want no complaints about it. We clear?"

Jax nods, his eyes wide. It breaks my heart into a thousand pieces to see him stare at Phantom like that. My son has never had a father figure in his life. Has never had even a grandfather. As much as I'm worried about what Phantom has in mind, I can't imagine he'd do anything to put my son at risk.

We walk into the living room, and Phantom motions for me to follow him upstairs. We go into his bedroom and close the door. As soon as we're alone, he pulls me close.

"We could have talked downstairs. I just don't know if I can stand another day without touching you."

I lift my face to his, and we kiss hard, need and desire unleashing themselves faster than I can believe. I never knew I had so much stored-up lust. But this man, his thick beard scraping my chin, his lips soft and hot against mine... His hips and the way he works himself against me when we kiss. I'm breathless, and my breasts are aching and raw when he pulls back.

"I can take Jax with me today," he pants. "I'm going to the compound. There won't be partying or anything unsafe. During the day, we've got guys sleeping, women cleaning and getting ready for the party—"

I have to trust him on that because we hear the girls pound up the stairs and slam the doors to their rooms. "That doesn't sound good," I say. "What's going on with them?"

"Mama drama," he says on a sigh. "Holly is worried about her mom and wants to talk to her. Daisy thinks we should wait until the court sets up a schedule. They're fighting over what Shayla's going to think when this is all over. Holly's stressed. I think a day at the mall will be good for them."

"What about tonight?" I ask. "Maybe I shouldn't go to the birthday party? Should we leave the kids alone?"

"I was thinking about that," he says. "Do you think your sister would want to come by and stay for a couple hours? We won't stay long, but still. I'm going to send at least one of my brothers to stand watch, but I'd feel better if there were someone inside the house too."

I nod. "I can probably get her to come by," I say. But

inside, I'm not convinced. I could get Clara to come, but I honestly don't trust that she won't ask the kids all kinds of inappropriate questions—like where I'm sleeping. That leaves just one person. "I'll make some calls," I tell him.

He nods, then cups my breast with one hand and tweaks my nipple through my bra. "So," he says, fondling and twisting me until my knees are weak, "am I rescuing your boy from the mall?"

"How can I say no to anything you ask right now?" I moan and lean into his touch, but he pulls his hand away, leaving me turned on and needy.

"That's the point, sweetheart," he says, giving me a wicked grin.

I swat his perfect butt and follow him back downstairs.

"Girls!" he yells. "Five minutes and Poppy leaves without you!"

Two sets of feet thunder down the stairs. "We're ready! We're ready!"

Phantom gives each kid a twenty-dollar bill. "This is for smoothies. Anything else you want, ask Poppy for permission." He hands me a wad of cash, but I refuse to take it.

"Phantom, I can cover whatever the girls—"

He holds up a hand and arches a brow at me. "I take care of my girls. All my girls." He wraps my fingers around the cash. "Get Stella something from me, too."

Then he leans forward and kisses me on the cheek.

"Well, well, well," Daisy says, crossing her arms over her chest.

"Well, well, well, what?" Phantom looks amused.

She holds a hand out to her sister. "I bet Holly that you would be boyfriend and girlfriend by the weekend. It's Saturday, so…"

Holly shakes her head and turns over the twenty Phantom just gave her. "I was making the point that adults don't really say boyfriend and girlfriend."

Phantom just smirks, and I put a hand on Jax's shoulder. "Listen to Phantom, okay? I'll see you in a couple of hours."

Jax nods so eagerly and enthusiastically, my eyes sting with tears. I'm not jealous or feeling left out because he is so, so excited for some time with Phantom. I'm grateful. I know I hardly know the man, but I have his daughters, and he has my son. I can't imagine a more profound expression of our trust in each other. He loves his girls more than anything on this planet, and he knows Jax is my everything. Sun, moon, and stars. I'm just grateful there's more than enough room in my universe for a few people to love.

———

Mom agrees to meet me, Holly, and Daisy at the food court for smoothies in an hour. I spend that entire hour in a total panic.

"What are you feeling for tonight?" Daisy's question startles me out of my worry fog.

"What? Hmm? Sorry."

Daisy frowns at me. "You seem weird. Is something wrong?"

I pinch my eyebrows together and frown. "My mom is interesting."

Daisy gives me a look like I'm completely stupid. And for a minute, I feel like I am. "Did you forget our mom tried to rob you? That Dad has a restraining order against her? How much worse could your mom possibly be?"

I immediately feel like the most insensitive idiot on the planet. These girls are going through so much with their mom right now. The worst thing my mother has ever done is judge me. Make me feel small and inadequate. As far as I know, she's never committed a felony. Never stolen anything. Never stalked anyone or put rats in their pool. But I've got to say, I'd love to see the look on her face if I asked about all that. I can't remember the last time my mom and I really talked.

I put a hand on Daisy's shoulder. "I'm sorry. You're right. What you're going through with your mom right now is really hard. My issues are nothing compared to that."

Holly grunts, and I swear I hear a bit of her dad in the sound. "It's fine," she pouts, sounding really annoyed. My God, teenage girls are a lot harder than ten-year-old boys. "You can have a shitty mom, and we can have a shitty mom. We all have shit. It's just life."

I nod and think about what she said. "You're right. My mom treats me like shit sometimes." I try not to apologize for cursing. It just felt right in the moment. "She wanted my life to be so different. She wanted me to marry a better guy, a richer guy. To go to college, have a good career."

"So, you didn't go to college?" Holly asks. "Why does that even matter? You own an awesome business."

"Yeah. I'd work there when I'm older," Daisy says. It's nice to hear them agreeing for five minutes. "Hair salons are so cool."

"That's what I always thought too. I still do. I don't have any regrets about that."

We wander toward the smoothie stand and grab an empty table with four chairs. The top of the table is sticky, but I know if I get up for napkins, I'll break the moment I'm having with the girls. I sit down and keep myself from touching the surface.

"Did your mom not like Jax's dad?" Holly asks. "Is it okay to ask that?"

I nod. "Yeah, of course. You can ask me anything."

"Good. So, you are my dad's girlfriend now, right?" Daisy interrupts. "Because I really like you, and Jax is cool. You should date my dad."

Holly rolls her eyes and huffs a hard, disappointed breath. "We were talking about something else, Daisy. Enough already. You won the bet."

"This isn't even about the bet. I want to know if she likes Dad."

"I like your dad," I assure her, grinning. "I wouldn't invite my mom here to meet the two of you if I didn't like your dad."

"I thought you wanted your mom to babysit us." Daisy looks confused, and Holly crosses her arms over her chest in barely contained disgust.

"Ignore her. Can we go back to what we were talking about, please?"

I scan the crowd of Saturday shoppers for my mom's distinctive white pixie cut, but I don't see her so I feel safe to answer. "My husband was my high school sweetheart. My mother thought I should date other men, experience life. Aim a little higher."

"What does that mean exactly?" Holly asks. "Your mom does sound kind of judgy."

I chuckle. "She can be. She means well, but..."

"Is she going to have a problem with our dad?" Holly looks concerned. "I mean, some older people still think tattoos are for criminals." She grows quiet as what she said sinks in. "And then there's that..."

She doesn't have to explain more. I reach across the table—stickiness be damned—and grab Holly's hand. I give it a quick squeeze, then release her. "Anyone who doesn't accept your dad doesn't have to have him in their life. But I want him in mine. And I accept him. All the parts of him."

"Well, I hope I get to meet him someday." My mother's voice, that tone. She's right behind me. And she's probably overheard a hell of a lot.

"Mom." I get up out of my chair and look over my beautiful, elegant politician mother. Lori looks like she just left a fundraiser and scored a massive donation. Her power suit is white, her heels are black and four inches high, and her blood-red-covered lips are turned down in a frown right now. "Thank you for coming."

I give Mom a stiff hug, but I can't help but notice how she looks from the sticky table to the girls, like she can't decide which she should clean up first. I ignore all the feelings of not being good enough that one scowl from Mom dredges up, and I turn the girls. They are smiling at my mom, looking at her with the same kind of wonder—and a trace of fear—Mom inspires at budget meetings.

"So," Mom says, putting on her work voice, "you must be the girls I've heard so much about."

I try not to flinch as she sinks the first dagger into my chest. The first Mom's heard about these girls was today, this afternoon when I asked her if she'd meet us at the mall. But the kids don't seem to register the insult, which is good.

Holly and Daisy stand and shake my mother's hand, which she offers to each of them like this is a networking event and the girls are future voters.

"Poppy, why don't you get something to wipe down this table while I get to know Holly and Daisy a bit better." Mom pulls out a chair and waves me off like I'm a member of her staff.

I sigh and run over to the smoothie counter to ask for some paper towels. I grab a few wet wipes from my purse, wipe down the table, then dry it with the towels while Mom asks the girls questions.

"Where do you go to school? And do you participate in any civic or community benefit clubs? Doesn't the high school have a group that sends singers to the senior center once a month?"

Holly and Daisy answer all her questions politely and with none of the anxiety or stress that Mom usually evokes in me. They're not seeing her questions as jabs, but as someone intensely curious about their lives.

Mom shakes her head and fluffs her pixie cut with

short, perfectly manicured nails. "You know, you're both old enough to start thinking about the impact you want to have in this world. Whether you want to make it a better place—" she throws a look at me "—or waste the time you've been given."

At that, the girls look confused, and the table falls silent. Way to go, Mom. Making a simple introduction about working for world peace.

I'm shocked when Holly asks, "What did you do when you were our age to make the world a better place?"

Her question isn't defensive or rude. She sounds genuinely curious about my mom's life. I take the girls' smoothie orders and excuse myself to go to the counter. I pull out my phone and fire off a text to Phantom.

> Me: Mom is giving the kids a lesson in community betterment. If they didn't hate me before, this might seal the deal. How's Jax?

I pay for the smoothies and read Phantom's reply while I wait for the order to be prepped.

> Phantom: Kid's a natural. I got him on one of the smaller bikes. Just a short ride around the parking lot, but we had a kid's helmet, so he's all good.

I reply a long line of exclamation marks and shake my head. I can almost guarantee that Jax would not get on a motorcycle even if Phantom invited him to. But then again, there are a lot of things I've done because

Phantom invited me to that I could never have imagined myself doing.

> Phantom: Fuckin with ya, babe. He's great. Drawing in my office while I make some calls. See you soon.

I love the text with a heart emoji, then carry the smoothie caddy back to the table.

"Small green goddess," I say, handing Mom her smoothie.

Mom takes it and thanks me, then takes a sip and continues talking with the girls. For the next fifteen minutes, she tells the girls about how she met my father at a protest on their college campus.

The smile on Mom's face as she talks about Dad makes me realize for maybe the first time how much my mom loved my father. I knew they loved each other, but by the time I was an adult, it was different.

Dad's passion for life and issues had been blunted by a career in a job he hated. He felt trapped, though, with two kids to support and a wife whose career was about optics and not about income.

It made me wonder if my mom, by pushing me to go to college, was really pushing for me to find someone like the man my dad was when she met him. Maybe what she wanted for me was something she was missing in her own life.

"Mom," I say, finally interrupting their conversation. "We should go. I need to pick up some gifts and a dress before the party tonight."

"What time should I arrive?" Mom asks. "Text me

the details and let me know if I'm making dinner for my grandson and his new friends or if we're ordering in."

"I'm sure we'll be ordering," Daisy says, smiling. "Pizza night."

Mom gives me a quick hug, then says goodbye to the girls. "I'll be looking forward to meeting the girls' father," she says.

The girls' father... Not my boyfriend, although, to be fair, I never called him that. But in that moment of my mother's careful choice of words, I can read between the lines. She's polite and interested in the girls, but no one, *no one* I pick will be good enough. Phantom has a lot to prove with my mother, and I feel like he's already failed the first test.

SIXTEEN
PHANTOM

WHEN POPPY COMES down the stairs in a little black dress, my cock and my heart leap to attention. The dress is formfitting and low-cut, so I get the best of both worlds—a view of her cleavage on top and her long, tanned legs below. Her hair is down and loosely curled, and she's carrying two small gift bags—one from me for Stella and the other from Poppy.

When she reaches the bottom of the stairs, the girls rush to tell her how pretty she looks, and I watch as they compliment her hair, the glittery shadow on her lids, and the soft pink lipstick.

She hugs each of them, and they have a private laugh about something I can't hear. I can only imagine what it was like watching their mother go out with her fucktoys. Douchebag guys looking for an easy hookup or a drinking buddy. I am damn sure that she never once went on a date looking like this.

I watch dumb struck as Poppy crosses the living room toward me. "Fuck," I grit out. I slide a hand beneath her hair and stroke the back of her neck with my thumb. What I want to do is pull her against me, shove that dress around her waist, and fuck her against the wall.

What I have to do is control myself.

Living with this woman has taught me more about self-control than my years behind bars.

The doorbell rings, and Jax jumps up from his tablet. He's been working on a project for me all day, something I had him start at the compound while I made calls. He runs to the front door with the girls, and they open the door to Poppy's mom, Commissioner Lori.

"Grandma." Jax hugs Lori, and she closes her eyes, rocking the boy back and forth in her arms.

"Hi, sweetheart. It's so good to see you. I met your new friends today at the mall. I heard you were out with Owen. Did you have a good day?"

"Owen?" Jax looks toward me, and I give him a look. I told him my real name was lame. "Yeah, it was awesome."

Lori gives my girls each a friendly hug, then strides right up to me with her hand out. "Owen," she says.

She doesn't say nice to meet you—because that would be a lie. She doesn't say good to see you again. Because that would give away the fact that Lori and I know each other.

We, in fact, go way back.

I look from Lori to Poppy and have to make the call fast. I assumed that Lori would have told Poppy she knows me when they met up at the mall today. But the way Lori's acting makes me think otherwise. Ordinarily, I would shake her hand and tell her to call me Phantom, but I don't, because I know that will only piss Lori off.

"Thanks for doing this," I say, shaking her hand. What I said doesn't reveal anything, and I'm even more careful with the look I give her. I don't know why the game matters. But I don't want to do anything to blow up this thing with Poppy, so I'm going to fucking play.

Lori turns her attention to Poppy, asking for a tour of the house and for any instructions she needs. Poppy explains about the pool being out of commission while I kiss the kids and text Hawk to make sure he saw Lori come in.

Once we've said our goodbyes to the kids, Poppy and I head out to the party. And I wonder just how long I can go without telling her about my dealings with her mom.

We arrive at the party early. We park in the lot, and I help Poppy out of the passenger side of my truck, taking the minute to hold her close to me.

"You look good enough to eat," I tell her. "Fuck this party. Let's go to my room and make a party of our own."

I kiss the side of her neck, the warmth of her hair and that gorgeous salon scent from her shampoo filling my nose. This isn't the stuff I bought her, so she must have picked up a bottle when she went back to work. My mouth waters, and I want nothing more than to bite her, lick her, taste every inch of this body as I peel the dress right off her.

Poppy sighs, angling her head to the side to give me

better access to her throat. "Phantom," she murmurs. "This is technically our second date. Are you expecting me to go all the way with you?"

"Hoping, begging, needing," I say, licking and suckling the tender, soft skin of her collarbone. "I want to be inside you, behind you," I grumble. But then I grab her hand and lead her over the gravel toward the front door. "Let's give these gifts away and fuck."

"The most romantic second date ever," she laughs.

I swat her ass as we walk through the compound door, and I immediately regret it because I don't want to move my hand.

The compound is decorated with a few streamers and balloons.

"Phantom." Penny runs up to me, her ass cheeks hanging out of her frayed denim short shorts. She's wearing glittery flip-flops and a skintight leopard-print tank top. "So, this is her, huh?"

Penny looks Poppy over from head to toe. "I hope you're not one of those snooty bitches." Penny's giving mean girl vibes, and I roll my eyes. This is a compound, not a high school clique. But Poppy works in a salon. She knows women. I cock a brow at Penny and stand back.

Poppy looks from me to Penny and gives her a confident smile. "If by snooty you mean sexy, that's the look I'm going for." She motions to her little black dress. "This is all for him, though, so I'll let you know how he likes it later tonight."

Penny cackles. "I like you. Come meet the girls."

Poppy turns to me, and I nod, waving her off. Penny

takes off toward the bar, and Poppy leans close to my ear. "Am I stupidly overdressed? Was this the wrong thing to wear?"

I cup her ass with both hands and pull her close to me. "Did you lie to Penny just now, or did you wear this for me?"

She laughs and leans her hips against mine. She laces her hands together behind my neck, her brown eyes blazing with heat. "Only for you," she purrs.

"Then who the fuck cares." I lower my lips to hers and kiss her so that every asshole in this compound knows she's mine.

She parts her lips and groans, melting into me until, finally, I have to let her go. I'm going to be tenting my fucking jeans all night if we keep at this.

She licks her lips and blots the smudged lipstick with her fingertips, then follows Penny to the bar. I hear Stella squeal, lots of hugs, and chatter. Shadow's at my elbow, holding out a beer.

"You got a minute?" he says.

I nod, and we retreat to a corner.

"Elliott's happy with the work. He's ready for another run," he tells me.

"What about the fuck who jumped King?" I ask.

"He still won't talk about it."

Ever since Dylan got jumped last week and beaten to within an inch of his life, I've been trying to put together the pieces. Somebody wants a piece of this Elliott gig. With this amount of money and product moving, that's just common sense. But there's nobody in town, no one that I know, who can put together the protection and power that we can. Something isn't adding up.

"You think he got side work?" I have to ask it. Dylan's been a prospect for over a year now. But time doesn't mean shit. Some guys will turn on their mother for a blow job, a snort, or a couple of bucks. You never really know someone until they've proven themselves —time and time again. Dylan hasn't done anything wrong—not that I know about yet. But that doesn't mean he has done enough right to convince me I can trust him.

"Been thinking that same thing." Shadow looks troubled. "We got a new gig, he's got a new hole in his mouth where his teeth were. You want eyes on him."

I nod. "I want to know everything. Who he talks to, who he sees. I want to know how bad his shit stinks if that's going to help us figure out what the fuck he's into."

Shadow nods. "Go back to the party. I'll cover this." He turns to leave but then stops. "How do you want to handle it if I see something going down?"

I down my beer, then set the bottle down and clench my fists. "You bring him to me."

Shadow wanders off into the crowd, but I see him kiss Stella on the cheek and then slip out of the party.

I walk up to the bar, frustration practically blurring my vision. I run this club with one rule: loyalty above all else.

Trust is everything.

I just hope that Dylan doesn't give me a reason to break any more of his bones.

"He's so into you." I overhear one of the ladies squealing at Poppy.

She's holding her own with the girls, slowly sipping a beer and looking comfortable at the bar.

"He is," I say, lacing an arm around Poppy's waist. "Happy bday, Stel," I say. "And thanks."

I nod, and Stella comes around the bar and squeezes my arm. "Poppy already thanked me like a hundred times. And this?" She fingers the silver necklace with a little birth month stone hanging from a silver charm. "Too sweet." She lifts up on her toes to kiss my cheek and whispers, "I know Poppy picked it out. She's a keeper."

Before I can keep her, I must have her, and that's something I plan on doing immediately.

I grunt at Stella and put a hand on Poppy's lower back. The music is pumping, and more bikers and bitches are filling in the compound. The TVs are blasting a game, and a couple of the guys are playing poker at a table.

"We're just about to put out the food!" Penny yells. "Let the birthday girl eat first, you fucks."

Poppy turns and looks at me, her eyes laughing.

"Having fun?" I ask.

"No one's naked or wasted yet, so I'm not sure what you warned me about," she teases.

"I have ideas about that," I tell her. I lace her fingers through mine and lead her back toward my room.

We're silent as we walk down the hall, the only

sound the pounding of my heart in my ears and the click of Poppy's heels on the tile. Once we're in my room, I shut and lock the door. The noise of the party fades away, and all that's left is us.

"Sit," I tell her, then open a mini fridge I keep beside the couch. "You want something, babe?"

She sits on the corner of the couch, feeling the soft leather. "No," she says quietly. "I'm good."

"You're better than good," I tell her, dropping down beside her. "You're fucking perfect."

"I like the girls," she says, a grin on her face.

I pop the top on another beer and take a drink. But then I set it down and look at Poppy. "We got a babysitter and a little privacy," I say. I'm about to tell Poppy all the shit I want to do to her when she stands in front of me and turns around so her back and ass are facing me.

"Zipper?" she asks, holding up her hair.

I stand and tug the zipper down, but I can't stop myself. I lower my mouth to her warm neck and kiss her soft skin. The scent of her hair, the heat of her body, sets my limbs on fire. My cock spears to life, and I press against her firm ass.

"Baby…" I drink in the scent of her, and it's like a fire ignites in my limbs and she's the water I desperately need. I reach around the front of her dress and cup her tits, squeezing them in my hands while I grind my cock against her. "I hope you like it hard."

I realize the minute I say it that might be the wrong thing to say. She stiffens, just a little, but I feel it, and I turn her around to face me.

"You want this?" I ask. "You want me? I don't know how much longer I can hold out. But I will. But you've got to tell me what you're thinkin', babe."

She swallows hard. "I'm scared to death," she says. "I want this. I want you. But I haven't had this with anyone in a long, long time. I'm just in my head."

If there's one thing I know how to do, it's get a woman out of her head. And it starts by getting her in my bed.

I take a step back and nod at her. "Take off your dress for me." She blinks fast but nods. I already undid the zipper, so she wriggles her shoulders from the straps and lets the black fabric bunch around her hips. She's not wearing a bra, and I swear to fuck, my favorite thing about this woman—after her mouth, her eyes, her everything—is those tits.

Her nipples go hard, the peaks dark brown and thick. My mouth waters to taste them, but I'm not going to make this quick. "All the way off," I tell her.

She shoves the dress past her hips, and it pools at her ankles. She steps out of it, then stands in front of me wearing only her underwear and heels. Her long brown hair has fallen forward to cover her tits, and while I like the mermaid-Venus look she's got going, I want to see her. I want to see everything.

"Move your hair and take off your panties." I watch as she nervously tosses her hair over her shoulders, then works the black silk down her long, thick thighs. I groan like a starving man before a feast when I see her thick curls. She's all natural, and I can almost smell her arousal from here.

"Leave your shoes on," I tell her. "Now turn around."

She does as I say and then kind of looks over her shoulder at me. "What now?" she asks, her voice raspy and thick.

"Bend over," I tell her. "Put your hands on my bed and spread your legs. I want to see you. Show me your ass, your pussy. Everything."

She does as I command, even wiggling her ass a little to show me she's getting into it.

I can't see much at this distance, but I've got her out of her head and focused on one thing at a time. "Good girl," I growl. "You're my good fucking girl, aren't you?"

I take a step closer and palm her ass. "This," I pant, puffing soft breaths against her ass cheek. "Is mine. I said I want you to show me what's mine. Show me, Poppy."

She moans softly, then climbs onto the bed. She lies back against the pillows.

"What?" I ask. "You going to show me how bad you want me, or do I have to take what I want?"

She doesn't say a word, but her cheeks bloom red and her lips part. "Look," she whispers. "Look what you do to me."

She opens her legs a little.

"Wider," I demand.

She obeys.

"Fucking wider," I bark, nearly feral with anticipation. "Show me what I do to you, Poppy. Show me what's mine."

She opens her legs and shyly puts her hand over her pussy. "I'm so, so wet for you." She says it quietly, but her eyes are molten chocolate. Her nipples are erect, and my cock leaps at the sight of her.

"You're not shy for me, Poppy. I know you're not shy." I stare at her pussy, arousal knifing through my gut. I want her. I want to claim her, part her legs and drive myself so deep into her heat that I lose my sanity. And I will. But she's got to be ready. She's got to want it.

"What should I do?" she asks.

I cross my arms over my chest and glare at her. "Show me what's mine," I demand again.

She moves her fingers, shyly at first, parting herself until I see the fucking promised land.

"I'm going to take what's mine, you hear me?" I ask.

She nods. "Phantom, please. I need…"

The words die on her lips when I drop onto the mattress and plant my face between her legs. I grip the sides of her hips and lap her, tasting every bit of wetness, every drop of her need.

"Fuck me, you taste good." I grunt against her mound, finding her clit and sucking it between my lips.

She groans and bucks, but I hold her firm, forcing myself to slow way, way down. I lick and suck her, trailing my fingers through her dense curls. I squeeze her thighs so hard I'm afraid I'll leave marks, but she presses her thighs open, wide for me, so I'm sure I'm giving her exactly what she wants.

She starts moaning, working her hips and clutching at my hair, but I'm not going to let her come so fast.

Using every ounce of my self-control, I pull my face from her pussy and lick and nibble the insides of her thighs.

"Phantom," she begs, "please, I need you. Need this."

I finally reach between her legs and slide my fingers against her soft skin. "Fuck me," I grunt, lost to anything but want and need. My body is on autopilot until I slide so deep inside her, I nearly come undone.

"Phantom," she moans out my name, but she goes weak, giving in completely to my touch.

Fucking finally.

I feel every ridge inside her, pistoning my fingers slow and steady. When I let her come, she's going to explode.

I start to feel her arc against me, her walls tightening and every breath ending in a whimpering purr, and I slowly slide my fingers out.

"No," she cries as I leave her alone on the bed, untouched and trembling. "What are you doing?"

I strip off my clothes in record time and grab a rubber from my bedside table.

"Wait," she says. "What about you?"

"That's a good girl." I grin. I toss the foil packet onto the bed beside her and climb up, my erection centered over her mouth. "I want to watch you suck me. Do you know how to suck cock, angel?"

She licks her lips, and I wonder for a second if I've said too much, pushed her too far. But she doesn't show any signs of pulling back. In fact, she moves one hand to cup my shaft and angles my dick toward her lips.

Lying on her back with me balanced on my knees over her, she licks and kisses my erection, swirling her tongue along the sensitive ridge under the head of my cock.

I try to keep still, letting her get used to my size, my body, but I've wanted this woman for too long. Waited too long for release. I feel my cock pulse, and I know I'm close, so I pull out and sleeve up.

"I want you to fuck me," I tell her. I drop onto the mattress beside her and lie on my back. "Ride me, take me, do whatever you need to come, but I don't want you to stop until you come."

"I don't know if I can," she says, a look of nervousness passing over her face.

I reach my hand between her legs and take some of the wetness from her pussy, then slip my fingers between her lips. "Taste that?" I ask her. "You want this, and it's yours for the taking, babe. I don't care if it takes all night. Fuck me until you come."

She swallows and licks herself from my fingers, and I pray to fuck I can hold out as long as she needs. She leans down and kisses my lips, then straddles my hips.

"You're in charge," I tell her, my hands at my sides. "You tell me what to do, and I obey."

"Squeeze me a little?" she asks.

"Where?" I ask. "Nipples? Tits? Clit?"

She pinches her nipples between her fingers. "Like this."

I reach up and gently take her nips in my fingers. I roll them between my thumbs and index fingers, slow and easy. I add a little pressure but no speed, just stroking and tweaking, working those tips until a bright flush blooms on Poppy's chest.

She swallows, her breaths coming fast, her eyes wide and full of intensity. She wants me. She wants this. And when she slides down on top of my cock, I have to hold back the roar that climbs up my throat.

She is tight, wet, and as soon as she's seated on my dick, I want to thrust hard, fuck her senseless. But I hold back. I want her to need this. To drive out the fear, the thoughts, the worries. The memories. I want there to be nothing between us. Nothing stopping or controlling what we are to each other.

"Fuck me, Poppy," I say, and I can't help if it sounds like begging.

She rolls her hips slowly over me, her thigh muscles tensing, her head thrown back. Her lips part, and she arches her chest forward, causing me to tug her nipples even harder. She whimpers, a gorgeous sound that's so hot with arousal, my cock leaps in response. But I control my breaths and just watch as she moves shyly at first. But then slowly, agonizingly slowly, she picks up speed.

She starts to grind on me then, lowering her hands to use my chest for leverage.

"Fuck me," I demand, begging, pleading, ordering. "Fuck me hard, Poppy."

Her nails claw into my shoulders, and I don't let up my hold on her nipples, tweaking, twisting, until finally, her whole body tenses and she opens her eyes to stare me in the face.

"I'm going to come," she tells me, and I take a hand

and pull her face to mine, opening my mouth and kissing her so every moan, every cry of my name, lands right against my lips.

I feel like I've waited a lifetime for this moment. A lifetime for this woman.

And we're just getting started.

SEVENTEEN
POPPY

I SAG onto his bare chest and do everything I can to stay out of my head. As soon as I lean my chest against his, he slides his hands under my hair and just holds me.

I don't know how long we stay like that, but once the fog lifts and I realize he's still inside me and he's still hard, I move my head so my chin is on his chest.

"I think it's your turn," I say.

His smile covers his whole face, and I see the hint dimples underneath his beard. I stroke his cheeks and sigh.

"Your turn," I hum against his chest. "It's your turn, Phantom. Are you going to…"

I can't say anything more because, in one swift move, he flips me over onto my back. I'm laughing and not even the least bit shy, even though I'm completely naked and just literally ground myself into his body like he's my personal plaything.

"You ready for my turn?" he asks. "Because I won't be fast."

I swallow and settle myself against the bed. "We have a babysitter," I remind him.

He grins but curses under his breath, then checks to make sure the condom's still in place. When he lifts my knees and hooks them over his elbows, then lines his erection up to my entrance, a spark of want blazes through me again.

"Phantom," I sigh.

"Poppy," he says. Then in an agonizingly slow thrust, he enters me inch by blessed inch.

I feel every perfect, amazing inch of his body as it enters mine. The way the head of his cock seems to nudge all the right spots. The way his shaft drags against my inner walls. I'm so lost to the sensations of his body inside mine, I don't even notice when he picks up the pace until my breasts are bouncing back and forth with every thrust of his hips.

"Roll over," he tells me, yanking himself from inside me.

I hate how cold and empty I feel the minute he's gone, but I do as he says, rolling onto my stomach.

"Ass up," he demands, holding on to my hips. I kneel on the bed and keep my face and arms on the mattress while lifting my rear end in the air. I feel a sudden smack of his palm against my bottom, and a rush of pleasure floods every cell of my being.

"Again," I beg, wriggling my butt against him.

He brings his palm down against my ass again, a soft slap sound echoing in the room. I cannot believe he isn't hurting me. Cannot believe the smack of his skin against mine sends a torrent of arousal from my bottom to my soul.

I rock back and forth slightly, my core so wet and needy, I feel like I could come again. It's been so long since I've been touched by anyone, and this is one hell of a way to break that seal. Phantom is ruining me for anyone else. Anything else. My fingers in the shower are going to be quite the disappointment after this.

Instead of another spank, I feel him palm my hips and guide me backward, closer to him. He slides his length inside me, then bends forward and cups my breasts in his hands. Using some kind of true superhero strength, he rockets his erection inside me, back and forth, in and out, until I see stars behind my closed eyes. My legs are boneless. My breaths are wild. My hair is tangled, and even my feet are cramping because I have never, I repeat never, been moved this way.

By the time I finish, Phantom is thrusting wildly into me. I'm spent. Exhausted. And yet somehow, I want more. I want this. Again and again.

How could I have ever been afraid? How could I have stayed away from pleasure, from connection, from touch?

I know how.

As Phantom collapses against my back, he rolls us onto our sides so he can tuck behind me and spoon me close to him. I close my eyes, not caring about my tangled hair, my sweaty back. I remember why I can't let anyone close to me.

Because when you find something this good, this powerful, losing it is like dying.

And I don't know that I have the strength to lose any more of myself.

It's not even ten o'clock when Phantom and I climb back into our clothes. We're both tired, satisfied, and yet, something feels different between us. Maybe it's me and my overthinking. I know that we've only known each other for a short time, but I know I could fall hard for this man.

What I feel for Phantom is unlike anything I've ever dreamed possible. More reason to protect myself. My heart won't withstand losing what it wants. Not again. Not this time.

We walk hand in hand through the compound, an awkwardness making my palms sweat.

"Poppy!" Stella runs up to me, looking adorable in some frayed black jeans and a sheer black top with a red bra underneath. "Come have drinks with the girls."

I look at Phantom, but he looks away. "We have to get back for the kids," I say.

Phantom leans forward and gives Stella a kiss on the cheek. "Happy birthday." Then he stalks off to talk to Viper.

Stella looks from me to him and back at me. "Uh, you two all right?"

I smile. "I'm tired. Sorry to be the party pooper. My

mom is with the kids, and we promised we wouldn't keep her out late."

Stella cups my face in her hands and gives me the happiest smile. "You are going to be great with him, okay?" She pulls me into a hug and whispers in my ear. "He's got it bad for you, Poppy. Sometimes he goes to dark places. Don't let him go alone."

She releases me and then turns and dances off toward the bar. I look for Phantom in the crowd. He's leaning against a wall, his arms crossed while he listens to Viper. He looks like he could beat the stuffing out of someone, not like a man who just came apart inside me. As if he feels me looking at him, he flicks a look at me. His nostrils flare, and unless I'm seeing things, his eyes sparkle.

He claps Viper on the shoulder, nods, then finds me in the crowd. "You ready?" he asks, taking me by the hand.

I'm so ready. Ready to find out how things went weird so fast and what I can do to bring us back to an hour ago, when he was my everything and I felt like, together, we were just right.

We walk through the parking lot to his truck, hand in hand. He opens the door, like he always does, and helps me in.

Once he gets inside, I turn to him. "Did I suck?" I ask him. "Was the sex bad?"

He blows air through his lips and rakes a hand through his hair. "Fuck no. I'd take you again right now in this truck if..."

"Then can you please tell me why you suddenly seem like you don't want me around anymore?"

Phantom pinches his eyebrows with two fingers and sighs deeply. He starts the truck but doesn't even put it in drive. He turns to face me, then turns away and stares out into the darkness of the sticky Florida night. "Poppy, I... *Fuck*," he hisses the last word.

He drops his hands roughly on the steering wheel, then grips it till his knuckles go white. He turns back to me.

"There's no easy way to say this." He looks wrecked.

"What is it?" My mind immediately starts doomscrolling, every horrible possibility I can imagine running wild inside my brain. "Do you regret having sex with me? I can go back home, Phantom. You don't have to—"

"I know your mother, Poppy, and she knows me."

I'm so surprised, I'm not sure how to react. "What does that mean? How do you know my mom?"

I try to think back to when I told Phantom my mom's name. He had seemed like he recognized it, but I assumed it was because a lot of people in our county know Mom's name.

"Phantom?" I press, the fears and anxiety starting to ramp into high gear. "How do you know my mother?"

He sighs. "She was on the parole board. The one that heard my case when I was incarcerated."

Oh. Whoa.

I have hardly told my mom anything, and yet she

already knows the ins and outs of Phantom's criminal past. Shit.

"Did she remember you?" I ask, trying to stay calm. "How long ago was it?"

"Years," he says. "And I'm pretty damn sure she remembers me."

"Why didn't she say something?" I ask. "When I met her at the mall with the girls, she didn't so much as flinch when I said your name. Did she put it together that you're the same guy?"

He nods. "I'm pretty sure."

I wring my hands, trying to stop the spiraling thoughts, but I can't stop the flood of words that come spilling out of my mouth. "Okay, so tell me, Phantom. What does this mean? You went to prison, I know about that. So freaking what. My mom's going to say what about it? She came over to babysit tonight, so she can't be too against you. Maybe she's over it. Maybe she doesn't care what you did then and is worried about who you are now. What happened at your parole hearing? What did she say when she voted against you? Are you going to hold it against her forever?"

"Poppy." He turns in his seat and looks at me, his dark-blue eyes ringed with sadness. "Your mother didn't vote against my release. She voted for it."

That, of all the things he's said, shocks me to my core. My law-and-order, by-the-book, politician mother voted for the early release of this man. "Okay," I say. "So again, I need you to dumb this down for me. What does this mean?"

He turns off the truck, and we sit in silence. "Poppy, I was denied parole the first time I tried. The second time, your mom was on the review board. I was asked to explain why I felt I wouldn't be a risk to the community. What I'd learned about myself while I was inside. What I could possibly offer the board as proof that I wouldn't eventually end up right back behind bars, wasting the taxpayers' money."

I swallow the lump in my throat as I listen. I can imagine my mother, with her perfect razor pixie cut, her sharp eyes, and her stern frown, looking over Phantom at his most powerless. I can imagine Mom demanding answers.

"What happened?" My question comes out in a whisper.

"I told them about Holly and Daisy. About Shayla. I told them that going away and leaving my ex-wife with babies wasn't the same as leaving them when they were old enough to understand what I'd done. To understand that they could only see their dad across a table once a month because I'd done bad things."

He's angry now and hurt. I hear it. All the years I've been fighting my mother's opinions, other people's disappointment, and my own pain, he's been fighting too.

"But she voted for you?" I ask.

He nods, opens his mouth, but then stops himself. I'm sure there's more. Knowing my mother, there's a zinger in there someplace. I just must brace myself for whatever shitty thing she said to him.

"Tell me, Phantom. I need to know everything."

He looks at me, and for a minute, I see something so honest, so pure in his face. If it were possible to believe, I'd call it love. "She told me about you, Poppy."

"Me?" I'm taken aback. "My mother talked about me in a parole hearing?"

"She was the first to cast her vote. Told me, looking right in my eye as she did it, that she was convinced I'd earned early release. She told me her daughter had lost her husband to a terrible accident and that she'd seen firsthand what losing a father does to a child. She said that even if I didn't give a shit about the community or the people I'd hurt, she believed I loved my girls. And if I cared about them as much as she believed I did, that I should think good and hard about the kind of man I wanted to be once I had my freedom. She said she knew her daughter would give years off her own life if that meant her son could have his father for even one more day. And she told me she expected great things from me."

Now, that sounds like my mom. I sigh and slump back in the seat. "Mom," I whisper. "She always knows how to cut to the goddamn bone."

"No, Poppy. Your mom was right. I haven't exactly lived up to the faith she put in me." He waves his hand toward the compound. "Getting out, having the kids, Shayla, dealing with child support and my parole terms. It was brutal. It was easier in some ways being on the inside, but I did the best I could."

I still don't understand all the ins and outs of the club, but I understood this much so far.

"Now I'm the club president. I make a fuckload of money. I've got my kids. But, Poppy, my hands aren't clean. Some of the shit we do ain't on the books. Any day could be the day I wake up and find out something we did went south. I'll go right back behind bars."

I don't say anything. I guess I'm not shocked to hear this. I mean, my client practically told me he was a criminal. But to hear that he could be in real trouble someday and go back to prison…

"That's partly why I divorced Shayla when I did. I wanted shit to be easy for her if I went back in." He looks at me. "I can't marry anyone, Poppy. I can't put a ring over the tattoo on your finger. If I did, I'd put you at risk. All I can ever offer you is less than what you deserve. And your mother will never fucking approve of me. Never. I will never be good enough for you."

I bark out a laugh. "Are you serious? You'll never be good enough for me because, what? You're not miserable like my dad, who slaved away at a corporate job and dropped dead a year after he retired?"

I shake my head. No little girl grows up thinking she's going to marry a guy with a criminal past—or a guy with a criminal present, for that matter. But I married a guy who I thought was right for me. I wasn't happy, and now he's gone. My dad wasn't happy, and now he's gone.

My mother didn't approve of Michael. She hates that I'm a stylist. So, what am I going to do? I'm thirty-five years old. Am I going to live the rest of my life exhausted, alone, and unfulfilled? I'm happy now. I've been happy ever since this tattooed, muscled biker walked into my salon to pick up his daughters. Since he took me into his house, his bed, and, I hope, his heart.

"I am not going to pretend I want a ring on my finger after the few weeks we've known each other," I say. "And I'm not going to say it doesn't scare me that I could lose you because of the work you do."

I look at him square in the eyes as I say it. "But I want you, Phantom. I want to stay in your house even though it makes no sense, because I *don't* want to leave. I love your kids and the way you listen to Jax. The way you make chicken soup. I am falling for you, and I don't give a good goddamn who doesn't like it."

I turn and look out the front window, but then I figure, you know what? Fuck it. I am tired of never feeling like enough.

So, I unfasten my seat belt, slide across the bench seat, and grab Phantom's cheeks with my hands. "I want this. I want you to make love to me again—no, to fuck me again like you'll never get enough. I don't care what my mother thinks of you. I don't care about Shayla trashing my house. I mean, I do, but only because that means I get to stay with you. I want you, Phantom. I only hope you want me too."

He reaches up and puts his hands on top of mine, and he is quiet for a long minute. He holds my hands against his face and closes his eyes. When he opens them, he looks resolute. "Let's go home. Starting tonight, you're sleeping in my bed."

I settle back into my seat and fasten my belt again.

The drive home is short and we're both quiet, but

the awkwardness is gone. Instead of me feeling like he's holding on to something, holding something back, I feel like we're holding on to each other. Our secrets. Our desires. Our truth. I'm prepared to fight for this. Even if that means fighting my mother.

EIGHTEEN
PHANTOM

WE PULL into my driveway just as I get a text alert from Shadow.

"What now?" I grab my phone and scan the message. As much as I need to be here tonight for Poppy and her mother, as soon as I read it, I know I have to go.

> Savage: 911. Dylan's house. Sending the address.

I groan and turn in my seat. "Babe, I got to run out. There's a problem with one of the guys who helped at your house. I don't know if it's related, but I have to go."

She looks stricken for a second, but then she nods. "You'll be back?"

"The second I can."

"And you'll be careful?" She looks like she doesn't want to ask that but can't help herself.

"Even more so now." I lean across the bench and

kiss her. "Tell your mom I'm sorry I had to run. Don't wait up," I tell her.

She kisses me back. Then she climbs out of the truck. I click open the garage and wait until she's inside, then I close the door again and tear off toward Dylan's.

My mind races as I drive, but I force myself to slow down. I drive past the house and see bikes and a couple of familiar cars, then park my truck a block away and run toward the house. When I get to the one with the right number, I pound on the door.

"Let me the fuck in," I growl.

The door opens, and Savage looks murderous. I step inside the house and am about to ask for an update when one look around the room stops me in my fucking tracks.

Dylan is lying on the couch, one eye swollen shut and bruised. His lip is split, and he's breathing hard through his mouth like it hurts to breathe through his nose. But that's not what's so shocking.

My fucking ex-wife Shayla is sitting on the couch beside him, and Viper's holding a 9mm to her head.

I motion to him. "What the fuck is that for?"

"I fucking told you." Shayla's on her feet the second the barrel isn't pointed at her head. She lunges at Viper, nails out, ready to claw.

Savage is on her in a second, pulling her arms tight behind her and neutralizing any threat to Viper. Viper's got veins bulging from his neck to his forehead. "This bitch is fucking tweaking," he spits. "And if she doesn't calm down soon, I'm going to put her ass in the ground."

"This bitch is the mother of my kids!" I shout, but then I turn on her. "So, she better have a good goddamn reason for being here. What the fuck is going on here?"

I grab Shayla by the blouse and pull her close to me. One sniff confirms what Viper said. She's coming down from something. The stink of withdrawal and the sickly-sweet smell of dope is practically oozing from her pores.

"You're going to settle the fuck down. You're going to sit still, and you're not going to hurt anybody in this room. You hear me? And if you answer all my questions, you won't leave here in a fucking body bag."

That silences Shayla fast. She glares at me then yanks herself from my hold. She drops down and sloppily moves close to Dylan. Oddly close. "You going to let him talk to me this way?" she screeches. "You're going to fucking put up with this from that loser?"

My blood is boiling. But it's not going to do me, my girls, or my club any good if I pop off. Not before I have answers.

I may not have any control over Shayla, but I've got something she wants. The kids. And as much as I refuse to let them be innocent pawns, if she doesn't want her parental rights revoked, she's going to give me the whole truth. "How long?" I demand. "How long have you been on fucking meth!"

Shayla whimpers. "I'm not, Phantom. I'm not, I just—"

I hold up my hand like I'm going to slap her. I won't —I've never hurt Shayla a day in my life, but the threat has an unexpected effect.

Dylan pops off. "Leave her the fuck alone!" Even with one eye and a busted lip, the kid's got balls. "Back off."

"What. Did. You. Say. To Me?" My words are lethally calm, and I stretch them out so he has to savor every one. "Repeat what you said. I want to hear you say it again." I take one finger and point at my face. "Say. It. To. My. Face."

Even with a black eye and a bruised face, Dylan has the good sense to look scared as shit. "Just leave her alone, man. All right?"

I pace back and forth in front of the couch, trying to piece this shit together. Viper's still holding his 9mm, but now he's pointing it at Dylan. Savage is standing back watching from the doorway, but his hand's on his waistband.

"Let me get this straight." I look to Shayla. "You've been using, I'm going to guess, what, eight, maybe nine months?"

"Phantom, you don't understand..." She tries to cut me off, but I give her a look and she clamps her mouth shut.

"Let me fucking talk," I tell her. "If you're going to lie to me, then we're going to sit here until we get to the truth."

I motion for Dylan to put his hand on the coffee table. "Right here," I tell him. "Like this. Starfish style. That's it."

He knows what I'm doing, and he doesn't like it. Doesn't want to comply, but I grab him by the throat and clamp my hands down hard.

"It's your neck or your fingers. You choose."

Shayla starts crying, and I throw her a look. "What is this asshole to you? Your dealer? What the fuck are you crying for?"

Dylan's got one hand spread open, palm down on the table. I pull a knife from my back pocket. "Now," I tell him, flipping the blade open, "you're down one eye, and that lip don't look too good. You want to lose a whole finger? Start fucking explaining."

"Phantom, please. Don't." Shayla's snorting hard now, snot and tears wetting her face.

Viper makes a disgusted noise, but I just hold up a hand. I've got this. Shayla is mine to deal with.

I take the blade of the knife and stab the tip into the coffee table, right between Dylan's thumb and index finger. "Start fucking talking."

Dylan reaches out with the hand not on the coffee table and puts it on Shayla's knee.

"So that's how it is," I say, nodding. Now, it's all coming into focus. "Jizz over here is your latest boy toy. He's the one you've been fucking around with. Leaving the kids alone so the two of you could get high."

Neither one of them denies it, and that's proof enough for me. But if Shayla's been fucking a prospect and the two of them have been doing drugs, that means the break-in at Poppy's...

It all comes together in my mind in a rush.

I sent Dylan to Poppy's to clean up. But he'd already been there because he was the one who broke in. Whether Shayla asked him to or it was his idea hardly matters. But I want to know.

"Whose idea was the break-in?" I ask.

"Mine," Shayla whispers, gripping Dylan's free hand with hers. "I asked him to scare that bitch who called you about the bill."

I draw in a furious breath and blow it out slowly.

"So, you're at my compound—" I point the tip of the knife at him "—drinking my booze and fucking my club bitches." At that, Shayla shoots him a look, and he just shrugs. "You know how it is, Shayla. A lot of willing pussy and no reason not to go there."

I've been there, done that so many times myself. But the look on her face makes it clear she had no idea he was fooling around on her.

"So, you were a guest in my house, and you decided it was no big deal to—" I stop pacing and bend to scream in his face "—fuck my ex-wife, then break in to my girlfriend's house."

"She's your girlfriend now?" Shayla scowls. "Fucking bitch."

"You don't open your damn mouth." I point the knife at Shayla. "You're sleeping with this douchebag and bringing him around my kids?"

"I never brought him around the girls," she says in a rush. "It was never about that, Phantom."

I ignore her and go back to pacing the floor, punctuating every question with the point of my knife.

I trusted Dylan. He was there the day Shayla confronted me about the kids at the compound. I remember now that he wanted to help, and I told him to keep his ass inside. He probably wanted to make sure

Shayla didn't say anything that would let me in on their little secret.

The brotherhood we have is based on trust. I know that I'd put my life in the hands of any one of these guys.

Viper, Savage, Shadow, Blade, Hawk.

They have my back, and I have theirs.

Not even one of them would fuck another man's ex-wife.

Not a single one of them would break in to an innocent woman's house.

We have honor.

We may be assholes, but we're only assholes with the assholes willing to play our game.

Dylan deserves what's coming to him.

"So, what," I scoff. "You little methheads are in love? You ransack Poppy's fucking house looking for shit to sell for drugs?" I'm screaming now, and I can't control my temper. I pick up the thing closest to me, a giant glass bong, and throw it against the wall. It shatters and splinters into a thousand shards on the floor. Some of the glass flies back at me and hits me in the arm. I don't care. I don't feel anything but rage.

Savage clears his throat, and I know he's giving me a warning. This is the beginning of an end, and I need to handle this like a leader. I will when I'm good and goddamn ready.

"How about those rats?" I seethe. "I knew whoever planted those fuckers had to have the security code to the pool." I point at Shayla. "That's all you. You think I don't know how many times the kids brought you over to swim, and this is how you repay me?"

"You tried to take her fucking kids, Phantom!" Dylan's visibly shaking now, and Shayla looks like she's going to be sick.

"I don't ever want to hear you talk about my kids. Do you hear me? You say their names, you even think their names, and I'll tear every last tooth from your mouth and stick them so far up your ass you won't be able to tell if you're eating or shitting. You got me?"

Viper cracks his knuckles. "I'm fucking done. These two gotta pay. Why don't you let me handle it? Two birds, one fucking bullet."

Shayla starts screaming and crying. "Don't! My God, Phantom. You'd let them take me from our kids!"

"You two pieces of shit killed rats and left them in my pool. You endangered the lives of our kids, not to mention violated the court's order. Breaking and entering. Felony damage to property. Who knows what other laws you broke. And why? Because in your cracked-out little skulls, you thought you'd scare Poppy for asking to get her bills paid?"

"It was the only way I could hurt you," Shayla says.

"What about hurting yourself?" I ask, suddenly mad as hell that she's on shit. "You were never an addict, Shayla. What the fuck happened?"

She doesn't answer, but her silence says enough. Dylan. Dylan's been into the shit since I met him, but I had no idea he was this far down the rabbit hole. A little weed, a little coke, who gives a fuck. But this?

"Who busted up your face?" I point at Dylan. "Because they sure as fuck didn't do nearly enough."

"I did it." Shayla was quiet. "It was me. I got mad after the rat thing. He was supposed to do it before the court appearance, but he said he couldn't get close to the house. I did it myself, and then…" She looks at me, real tears in her eyes. "Then I beat him with a rolling pin. I don't know what came over me. I'm so angry all the time. I feel sick. I'm scared."

She's got spit in the corners of her mouth, and for the first time, I can see how truly broken she is. It softens my heart to see, but just a little. Not enough to put my knife away.

"You're right, Phantom. It's the drugs. I'm not myself. I haven't been myself for a long time." She drops her face into her hands and sobs. This time, unlike before, the tears are real. "I can't do it anymore. I want to stop. I just can't."

Dylan puts an arm around her shoulders and pulls her close. I gag a little in my mouth, but I just shake my head. And then I make a plan.

A plan that's going to get me, my girls, and Poppy the life we deserve and the peace we want.

By the time I get back home, I'm exhausted. The house is dark and quiet, but the television is on. Poppy is curled up on the couch, watching a movie on silent with just the captions. As soon as I come inside, she jumps from the couch and throws herself against my chest.

She doesn't ask anything, and I don't say anything.

I lean my chin against the top of her head and breathe in the expensive scent of her hair. She laces her hands behind my back and holds me like we've been doing this for years and not weeks.

It's way too soon to feel that I love her, but I love this. Who she is. How she holds me. The fact that she is here. I love *this*. I didn't want to go back to the compound, join the party, drink myself sick, and sleep with anybody willing and warm.

I don't know if I'll ever be able to do that again. Not if Poppy's waiting here for me.

I click off the television and lace my fingers through hers. We climb the stairs, passing by the kids' closed doors. Everything is quiet. Everyone is asleep.

"I need a shower," I tell her once we're in our room.

"Alone?" she asks. "Or do you want company?"

As tired as I am, there's never a time I'll say no to this woman. "Come on."

I turn on the taps, and we strip out of our clothes. I stand under the spray and let the hot water hit the top of my head.

"Come here." She motions for me to step out from under the water. She turns off the faucet and flips the dial so the tub starts to fill. She sets the shower curtain outside of the tub and sits down, gesturing for me to sit in front of her.

I do as she says, positioning myself between her legs. She drips a handful of shampoo into her palms and gets to work massaging and soaping my head.

"Sweet Jesus," I tell her. "No wonder people pay an arm and leg for this. You're incredible."

She laughs, and I rest my hands on her knees while she scratches and massages my scalp. We don't talk, the sound of the tap filling the tub the only sound in the room.

"Are you hurt?" she asks quietly. "You're bleeding, Phantom."

I look down at my arm and notice the places where I picked glass from my skin are dotted with dried blood and a couple of gouges.

"It's nothin'," I tell her. "I'm all right."

She doesn't press me, and I'm grateful. I don't want to talk. I don't like what I felt tonight. I have to be careful now because I have people to be careful for.

After she's done with my hair, she works the shampoo deep into the knots in my neck. It feels so good, I just want to sleep. Let my head roll back and lose myself in her touch. But the bathtub is full of soap and blood, dirt and sweat, and I feel relaxed but not clean.

"Let's rinse off," I tell her. I take her hand, and we stand. I drain the tub and flip the showerhead back on. We rinse off, wrap ourselves in towels, and climb into bed slightly damp.

The lights are off, and I make sure the house is armed. Then I shut off my phone. Stella's party is still in full swing, no doubt. There's nothing anybody's going to need me for, and if they do, fuck 'em.

Under the covers, Poppy snuggles against me, her

damp hair sticking to my chest. I don't even mind. It smells sweet and expensive. Like her.

"Talked to my mom tonight," she says softly.

I grunt. I'm sure she wouldn't tell me about this if the news wasn't good. I'm clearly in no mood for any more bad news.

"She thinks you're sexy." Poppy laughs. "A little weird coming from my mom, but she's not wrong."

I let myself smile at that. "Hmmm."

"And," she continues, "she said she's proud of you."

My eyes fly open at that. "Come again."

"She's proud of you. She knows who you are, Phantom. She knows about the club, what you all do. I guess you have a reputation around town."

I do have a reputation, so I can't imagine what the fuck Lori Davis would be proud of me for. If it's worth telling, I'm sure Poppy will share it.

She doesn't say anything more, though. She presses her ass against me, and my cock takes notice.

"You going to tell me?" I ask. "Or should I fuck it out of you?"

She moans, a deep, sexy sound, and the blood in my entire body shoots straight to my cock.

"Is that last thing an option?" she asks. "You're tired."

I say nothing. Just nudge her ass cheeks with the head of my massive erection. "More than an option. Now, it's a need."

"Will the kids hear?" she asks.

"Depends on how loud you scream." I roll over and grab a condom from my bedside table. The lights are out, and with the room-darkening curtains, I can't see her gorgeous eyes, her damp curls. But I can feel the curve of her hip, the ways she shifts her weight and sighs as I lie on my side and slip my hand between her thighs.

"Your clit is my new favorite thing," I whisper, stoking her,

I cover her mouth with mine, kissing her until she whimpers. I slide the condom on and feel between her legs. She's soaked for me.

"My good girl," I breathe the praise against her lips. Then I kiss her, flicking my tongue against hers, tasting her as my cock slides in deep, seating myself as far inside her as I can go, and then I drag my cock out slowly, making sure she feels every single inch of me. She gasps, and I cover her mouth with mine. "Shh," I remind her. "That's a good girl. Take all of me."

I jerk my hips hard, thrusting so deep she thrashes her head against the pillows. I feel her legs wrap around my hips and her feet dig into my ass cheeks, pulling me closer. Deeper inside her.

"Good girl," I mumble, my vision going dark as I close my eyes and focus on long, slow, deep thrusts. I piston my pelvis, every muscle in my body burning as I try to control my movements. The bed doesn't creak; Poppy doesn't cry out. We're silent, and yet between us, there is a fucking parade of sound and sensation.

I know I'm hitting the right spot when Poppy's hands claw my back greedily. "Phantom," she whimpers, her voice little more than a gasp. "You feel so good."

"How do you want to come for me?" I ask.

She writhes beneath me, working her hips to meet my every thrust. But then something feral unleashes in her. She's gasping and digging hard at my back, lifting her hips like she's grinding out an orgasm against my body. I feel her tits smash against my chest, and I lower my mouth to hers again, kissing her lips until our teeth bang together as we fuck.

It's nasty and needy, hard and quiet. Restrained and yet totally out of control. I don't bother holding back. I come hard, shaking and dripping sweat onto her. I feel her walls clench as I come, and she's falling apart beneath me, shuddering and panting, her heavy breaths the only sound she allows herself to make. My good girl.

I want to smack her ass, lick her cunt. Taste her, touch her, and do every godforsaken thing she'll let me do. But not tonight. Tonight, I'm going to hold her close and fall asleep with her hair tangled on my pillows.

Tonight, I'm going to sleep with the woman I'm going to make mine forever.

Knowing that, I'll be able to rest easy. We've got all the time in the world.

Pretty soon, we'll be free.

NINETEEN
POPPY

Mondays have become my favorite day. I get up in the morning and take the kids to school, then Phantom comes home, and we make love until he picks the kids up. Sometimes, he goes to work, and other times, he stays with me, and we spend hours in bed.

Today, though, won't be a lot of fun.

So much has happened fast over the last few weeks. Dylan, the prospect behind the break-in at my house turned himself in to the police. After some tough conversations with Phantom, he admitted to the break-in, the destruction of my property, the break-in here, and the rats in the pool. Both Phantom and I pressed charges, and due to some other minor stuff on Dylan's record that he was on probation for, he's waived a trial and negotiated a plea deal. He will be moved to the state prison to start a term of fifty-four months with the possibility of parole in twenty-four.

I cleared out my house and am fully moved in with

Phantom. It's fast, but I have a tenant renting my place. It's a good investment, and I'll hold on to the house just in case I ever need or want it back.

Jax loves his new room and has settled into having stepsisters. He and Daisy are the best of friends, and my mom has come to dinner a couple times. I don't know what she knows about Phantom's work, and I don't ask. She seems to absolutely adore him, and that's more than enough for me.

Even more amazing is how Mom has taken to Daisy and Holly. While she was strict and downright mean to me and Clara, she loves the girls. So much so that she's paying for a night in a fancy hotel for all of us tonight, including Mom. Mom will stay with Jax in one room, the girls in another, and Phantom and I in a third. Clara is covering the salon for me tomorrow so I can take the day off. No one is more excited than my baby sister that not only am I doing something for myself, but that I'm doing it with Phantom. She might just be his biggest fan. After me, Jax, and his daughters, that is.

I've appreciated their support over the last few weeks. Most surprising is the support coming from my mom. We're all going to need a little break after today. A little extra time as a family.

We kept all the kids home from school. Jax is up in his room playing, and the girls are on the couch waiting nervously. My mom is already at the hotel and has a dinner reservation for us at a beachfront restaurant. Now, all we have to do is wait.

I pad down the stairs and drop on the couch between the two girls. I stroke the faded blue streak in

Daisy's hair. "We could touch this up or try something new."

Daisy shrugs and sniffles, then drops her head on my shoulder. "Thanks, Poppy."

Holly is texting away, not looking up but clearly listening. "I was thinking about color," she says quietly. "Maybe pink. Do you think I could pull off some pink?"

"Absolutely," I tell her. "We'll go over samples when we get back. We can do it over fall break if you want."

Holly looks up at me, tears in her eyes. "Thanks." Then she sucks in air, and I have to resist the urge to look at her phone.

"What's with you?" Daisy snaps.

"I'm excited, okay. Tyler just asked me if I have a date for the winter dance."

I smile. "You guys just went to homecoming, and he's locking you down for the winter dance? When is that, like January?"

"Yes," Holly says, blushing furiously. "That's not normal, right? I mean, why is he asking me now?"

"I think he's trying to say he wants to still be dating you in what, three more months?"

"It's like two and a half," Daisy says, sounding bored. "Whatever. I'm over Tyler."

Holly rolls her eyes. "You can't be over him. Can you just try to be supportive?"

Before an argument can break out, we hear the sound of the garage door opening, and both girls fall silent.

"Hey," I tell them, putting a supportive hand on

each of their knees. "It's going to be okay. Come on. Grab the albums."

The girls grab the books they've made with some help from Jax, and we stand, waiting for the door to open. When it does, Phantom comes in first, followed by Shayla.

"Mom." Holly collapses into tears and runs to grab her mother.

"Baby." Shayla wraps her arms around her daughter and rocks back and forth. "Oh, my sweet, sweet baby."

Daisy throws herself onto the pile but isn't quite as emotional as Holly. Phantom walks up to me and wraps an arm around my waist. He silently kisses my forehead.

"Okay, okay, enough of that. Let me say a proper hello to Poppy." Shayla releases the girls, but she holds their faces in her hands and kisses their foreheads. "Poppy, would it be weird if…" Then she comes over to me, hesitating like she wants to hug me.

"No, of course it's okay." I open my arms and give her a quick hug. "Let me call Jax down to say goodbye."

"It's okay," Shayla says. "You don't have to bother him."

"No, it's all right. He'll want to say goodbye." I walk over to the stairs and call for Jax to come down.

Meanwhile, Shayla sits with the girls on the couch. "So you're going to be able to write to me," she says. "And the case worker I talked to said, depending on how I'm doing, I might even be able to make calls." She looks at Phantom. "I'll coordinate any calls through you first. I don't want to disrupt what you've got going on here."

Phantom doesn't say much. He just nods. "Whatever you want, Shay."

It's been a rough eight weeks for the kids. After Dylan turned himself in, Shayla spent two weeks in rehab but then relapsed. She overdosed twice during that time, and it was Phantom and Savage who picked her up and checked her in to an inpatient program. That seemed to work. She's been accepted into an immersive three-month rehab program in California. Phantom has given her the money for it.

If Shayla is clean and sober, she can have a relationship with her kids. If she can't stay clean... Well, as a mother, I don't want that for her or the girls.

The kids give their mom the cards and photo albums they made for her to take to California. Holly is an emotional wreck, and Phantom and I have already set up some counseling for her to help her navigate the next few months. She's got a lot of guilt about what's happening with her mom, and making sure she deals with it as best she can is both of our top priorities. That's why Mom booked us a one-night getaway and why we kept the kids out of school.

After Phantom and the girls drop Shayla at the airport, we're going for a one-night family staycation. We'll eat dinner on the beach, play games, and get our minds off the fact that Holly and Daisy won't hug their mother again for at least three months.

Jax bounds down the stairs, and he waves a polite hello to Shayla.

"Hi, sweetheart. Thanks for coming down." Shayla nods at him and then tells her daughters to be good to their new brother. "You always wanted a brother. You couldn't ask for a better one, huh?"

Daisy nods, and Holly starts crying again.

"We should roll," Phantom says quietly.

Shayla nods and gets back up from the couch. She walks straight up to me. "I know I wrote that letter when I was in detox," she says. "But I have something I want to say to you."

I look at Phantom, and he shrugs.

"Of course," I say. "What is it?"

"Just thank you. I'm sure you can imagine, if you were in my shoes…" She stops as tears start running down her cheeks. She blots them with her palms and keeps talking. "Maybe you wouldn't do drugs and would never have an addiction like this. But if you had to leave your kids. If you got sick or hurt…"

"Shayla," I say. "It's okay. I love them. As their dad's girlfriend and their friend. They'll only ever have one mother. But I'll be here for them until you can be."

She nods. "Thank you, Poppy. For everything."

Then she turns to Phantom. "I appreciate the ride."

He grunts, and then Daisy and Holly grab their mom's luggage, and the three of them head for the garage. Phantom stays behind with Jax and me.

"You cool?" he asks.

"Completely," I say.

And it's true. After my son lost his dad, I couldn't imagine not being supportive of a woman who's doing everything to get herself together. She might never have full custody of the girls again, but she's been talking about a new career, a new direction for her life. Maybe she's tired. Maybe she just needs a break from being a full-time single mother. I'm so grateful to be able to carry some of that load.

Phantom leans down and kisses me. "Love you. Be ready to hit the road when we're back."

"I love you," I tell him. "We will be."

Jax turns and heads upstairs. "Mom, can Ryan sleep over this weekend?"

"Did you ask Phantom if it's okay?"

"Yeah, he said it's fine."

"I'll text Tera and ask."

He bounds upstairs, leaving me alone. I walk into the kitchen and stare out over the back of the property. The afternoon sun glitters on the water in the channel, and the pool, completely clean, sterilized, and back in use, sparkles in the sunlight.

I rub my thumb along the tattoo on my ring finger.

Grief is a funny thing. How long is long enough to hold on to feelings of sadness?

———

After we check in to the hotel, we get the kids settled in their rooms, and Phantom and I shower and change for dinner. Phantom makes calls on the balcony of our room while I get ready, so once I'm done, we trade places.

I stand outside and peer out over the beach, watching the sunset. I feel so many things tonight. I've been thinking about Michael a lot lately. Not in a sad way. I don't miss him—not in the ways I used to.

I wonder if he can see us. If he knows how happy I am. How strong and funny, smart and talented Jax is. If he knows that he'll always be Jax's father and my first husband.

"Babe." I feel Phantom come up behind me and wrap his arms around my waist. "You ready?"

I haven't told Phantom that today is the nine-year anniversary of Michael passing away. He has enough to deal with getting Shayla off to rehab, keeping the kids calm. I'm okay; I really am. But I've realized over the past two and a half months that the exhaustion I was feeling might have been, at least in part, because I'm carrying so many memories. Ghosts feel scary and shapeless until you try to hold one in your heart. Then they just become heavy. And so, so sad.

I turn to Phantom, but I must swipe at a few tears that wet my cheeks.

"Hey." Phantom pulls me close. He holds me against his chest and doesn't say anything. I just breathe in the scent of him, feel the heat of him, the strength of him. He's become my safe and happy place. With him, a grunt can mean everything from fuck off to great job. A single look can say everything. But when it matters, when I need him to, he knows just what to say. "This is all a lot. Thank you for going through this with me."

I hug him hard, then reach up and stroke his beard. I don't say anything either. I know that he knows what's in my heart. What was there is moving, shifting, getting smaller to take up less space. The love I feel for

Phantom and the girls is growing to fill the space with something lighter, something vibrant and alive.

I put on a big smile. "Let's get the kids."

Mom and the kids are waiting for us in the lobby of the hotel. The girls are dressed in cute sweaters and jeans, and Daisy's wearing new pink high-tops that Jax helped her decorate. Daisy loops an arm through mine and practically skips out onto the terrace. Mom walks with Jax, and Phantom has his arm around Holly's shoulders.

Once we're seated, the server takes our drink orders and hands out menus. "I don't know if they told you when you made the reservation," the server says, "but there is a small wedding in the hotel tonight. Just sixty people in one of our smaller ballrooms, but you might be able to hear some music if you're still out here in about an hour."

"What kind of music?" Daisy asks, and Holly shoots her a look. "I just want to know. I mean, if it's good…"

Phantom chuckles and reaches for my knee under the table. I slide a hand down to cover his and stroke the tops of his knuckles while I skim the menu. We order our meals, and the mood is quiet. Holly and Daisy don't seem to have the energy to bicker, and Jax seems to know no one's really in the mood to talk.

Mom keeps up a constant flow of conversation, which I actually appreciate because it's different, not the usual school and work drama. When the kids want to order dessert, Mom pipes up, "Dinner's on me." She smiles at Phantom and me. "If it's okay with your parents, everyone's ordering dessert."

I give Mom a look, wondering why she's doing all this. Is she just trying to make up for the lost years we had when Jax was tiny and I couldn't do things like dinners or trips? I don't know if she knows the date today. I know Jax doesn't know. That's one thing I didn't want to burden him with as a child. We don't celebrate his dad's heavenly birthday or the day he passed away. I do that quietly, by myself. It just seemed cruel to, twice a year, make a child be reminded of what he'll never have from a man he doesn't remember.

It's not like I hid the dates from him, but he's never asked. Someday when he's older, I will ask if he wants to know. If he does, it'll be his choice how to celebrate or whether to observe the dates at all. But I'm sure Mom knows. Just like I'll never forget her wedding anniversary with my dad, the story of how they met.

While we eat dessert, music does travel from the hotel ballroom out onto the terrace. It's typical wedding-reception music, intended to get people up and dancing. It seems to do the trick for Mom. As soon as she finishes her last spoonful of crème brûlée, she pushes back her chair and heads for the little gate that separates the dining area from the beach.

She kicks off her shoes and motions for the kids to join her. "Come on, Jax. Dance with your grandma."

Jax looks at me like Mom has lost her mind. I call out, "Mom, that gate locks so people don't wander in from the beach. If you go out, someone's got to stay back here to let you in."

Mom's got her heels in one hand, and she's already working her hips, moving closer toward the water in time with the music. "Don't care," she says. "I put dinner on my room, and I've got a room key."

Jax looks to me for permission, which I give, and to my surprise, he takes off onto the beach with his grandma. He kicks off his shoes and runs back and forth, picking up shells and wiggling his toes in the surf.

Phantom looks at his kids. "What about you two?"

"What about you two?" Daisy mimics her dad's gruff voice, and I burst out laughing.

He lifts one brow at her and growls, but she just takes her sister's hand and says, "We're going."

Holly, to my surprise, lets her little sister drag her onto the beach. Daisy immediately starts dancing with Mom, kicking up her arms and legs like a loon. Holly has the good sense to look embarrassed for about five seconds, but after glancing around and seeing there's only a handful of people in the restaurant and our family dancing on the beach at sunset on a cool, late-fall night, she grabs Jax's hands and starts spinning him in circles.

Mom is a one-woman dance party out there, leading the kids in what looks like a lot of fun. I sip the last of my wine and watch them, absently rubbing my finger over my tattoo.

"I can't decide if I want to join them or ditch 'em," Phantom says as he looks out over the beach.

"Same," I laugh.

The stars sparkle over us as the night grows later, the sky as dark blue and brilliant as Phantom's eyes.

"Both?" he asks. "One dance then back to our room before we get dragged into the game room or a movie?"

I get up from the table and take his hand. I kick my heels off once we hit the sand, and Phantom toes off his motorcycle boots. We leave them by the restaurant gate, and Phantom puts his hands around my waist. I wrap my arms tight around him and rest my cheek against his shoulder.

We sway to the music while our kids jump and dance around us. Mom's white hair glitters under the moonlight.

I look up at the stars and, instead of imagining Michael, see midnight-blue eyes. The deepest smile. A black beard that tickles my cheek when he lowers his lips to kiss me.

I say a little prayer for Michael. I hope he's at peace. I hope he knows that, just like Holly and Daisy saying goodbye to their mother, goodbye doesn't mean you stop loving the person. Not having them in your life every day doesn't mean there isn't still room for them in your heart.

I must let him go. Once and for all. I have to release the love I once had and embrace the love I do have.

This isn't goodbye forever, I think. *This is just what it looks like to finally heal.*

———————

By the time we get up to the room, even the wedding music has stopped. My toes are sandy, and the kids are sweaty. Mom agrees to let the girls watch a movie in the room she's sharing with Jax, and she assures me she'll get Holly and Daisy to bed after the movie.

She lets the kids get off the elevator first, holding back a little while the girls and Jax run off toward their connected rooms. She turns to Phantom. "I'm learning to be a little more like you," she says. She gives him a long hug. "Sometimes you don't need to say anything, but you've communicated so much."

When she pulls back from the hug, she reaches up and cups his face, nods, and then turns to me. She gives me a hug as well, and I thank her for everything.

When she pulls back, I see something in her eyes. Tears. "This may not be the life I pictured for you," she says, "but that's okay. It's better than even the best I could have imagined. I'm proud of you."

Then she runs, still barefoot and holding her heels, down the hallway after the kids. "Wait up," she yells. "Grandma Lori smuggled in microwave popcorn!"

Phantom looks at me, his eyes wide.

I just shake my head.

"I have absolutely no words," I tell him.

We hold hands and head to our room. Inside, we're both quiet. Unusually quiet. I'm sure he's got a lot on his mind with Shayla and sending her off to rehab. My mind and heart are full too. I wash off my sandy toes in the bathroom and change into a sleep tee and shorts. I brush my teeth, then join Phantom on the balcony. He holds me and looks out over the water.

"I love you," he says quietly. "You know that, right?"

I nod. "I love you too."

"Kids are down the hall. Can't hear a thing. You want to fuck?" he asks.

I look up into his face, giving him a wide-eyed stare. "Are you serious?" I ask him. "We're wasting time."

He scoops me up in his arms and carries me inside the room. He sets me on my feet as soon as we're inside the sliding glass door and leans me against the wall. He lowers his mouth to mine and kisses me gently, his mouth exploring mine. He tastes like wine and dinner and that intoxicating combination of his scent. I fumble my hands all over his body, grabbing his back and pulling him closer as our kisses grow more intense.

Our tongues tangle, and my body thrums to life, all sadness and memories safely packed away in the small space I'm going to keep for them. All I can see is Phantom, this life, and possibilities. All I can feel is his love. And his incredibly hard cock pressing against his fly.

I reach down to unzip him, and he yanks my top over my head. He drops to his knees to tug off my shorts. While I'm standing pressed against the wall, I spread my legs wide enough that he can fit his face between my thighs. He kisses the tender skin of my inner thighs with his mouth, scraping and scratching my legs with his beard, his chin driving me into an aroused frenzy.

I love his friction. His hard and soft parts. His groans and nibbles, growls and kisses.

He stands again and scoops me up, carrying me to the bed. He takes all his clothes off while I watch, appreciating his muscles, his tattoos. The dark hairs that cover his legs and chest.

"Open for me," he demands, and I do.

I lie back and spread my legs, and he dives between my thighs. He takes his sweet time on me, first kissing my thighs more until my clit is throbbing with need. When he finally sweeps his tongue between my legs, I gasp. He sucks my clit into his mouth and slides two fingers inside me, working his way through my wetness to stroke the tender spots deep within my body.

I lie there boneless, taking in all the pleasure he wants to give me. My eyes are closed, and I let the already familiar bliss transport me to a place where there are only the two of us. Him, deep inside me, as close to the most intimate parts of me as anyone can be.

"I want it rough." I struggle to get the words out through my heavy breaths. "Fuck me hard, Phantom. I want to feel everything," I pant, coming so close to going over the edge just from his tongue and fingers. But I don't want to fall apart just yet.

He slides on a condom that I didn't even know he had and then spreads my legs wide open.

"Better than dessert," he says.

I groan. "Better than crème brûlée?"

"Ever damn day of the week."

He enters me slowly, rocking his hips and sliding his cock deep inside me, taking his time. He's kneeling so he can watch himself enter my body. His lips are parted, his eyes dark, but he doesn't speed up. Doesn't fuck me hard until I can't think or see. Until I can't tell if I'm numb or feeling everything.

"Get on top and fuck me," he says.

He sits at the top of the bed with his legs straight, and I climb over his lap. The hotel bed has a headboard, so I grip it with my hands. That puts my breasts right at mouth level, and Phantom doesn't hesitate. He sucks my nipple into his mouth hard, the exquisite pleasure tinged with the tiniest edge of pain.

I need this. Need him. Need to push out the power and emotion that are inside my body. I grab the headboard harder for leverage, and with Phantom's mouth still sucking, I start to ride him.

I move slowly at first, finding just the right spot, but once I feel it, the length of him inside me, the base of his shaft putting the perfect pressure on my clit when I roll my hips, I move faster. A wild need unleashes inside me, and I thrust hard against him. I yank the headboard hard and power my body against his, harder, faster, until the headboard bangs rhythmically against the wall with every brutal jerk of my hips.

"Don't stop." Phantom's panting hard against my breasts, his hair flopping as I work out my need, my desire, my frantic chase for bliss against his body. "Fuck yes, Poppy."

When I finally come, the climax builds so fast, hits me so hard, I cry out. My nipple is still in Phantom's mouth, and I'm still moving, shaking, grinding, lost to bliss, fullness and emptiness all at the same time.

I realize as I slow down that he's coming too, emptying inside me. He curses under his breath and bangs his head back against the headboard, his hips lifting to meet mine. When the orgasms fade, I stay on top of Phantom, sweaty and breathless. My wet chest sticks to his, and I bury my face against his shoulder.

"That was a first," he says, his voice sounding a little shocked. "Am I a bottom now?"

I let out a weak giggle. I feel too good to think. Too good to analyze. "As long as we can do that again, who cares?"

"I'm going to need a minute, but fuck yeah." He helps me and my exhausted legs off him, peels off the condom, and we spoon together naked under the blankets.

"You're the best thing to ever happen to me, Poppy," he says. Then, immediately, he starts to snore.

I smile and close my eyes, listening to him breathe. I used to be exhausted by life in the worst possible ways. Everything felt hard, and I never felt good enough to live up to even the lowest expectation. I fall asleep smiling and exhausted in the best ways.

I'm full of love.

I'm happy.

I'm finally starting to believe it.

TWENTY
PHANTOM

MY PERSONAL LIFE may be in great shape right now, but the business has gone to shit. Turns out that fucking tweaker Dylan stole a shit-ton in product during the job we did for Elliott. Savage caught him and recovered almost all of it, and that was the leverage we needed to get him to turn himself in for the break-ins, the rats, everything. I told him if he didn't go away for a while, I'd let Viper make sure he went someplace he'd never come back from.

While the situation is under control with Elliott, I'm feeling less sure about my brothers.

"We need to diversify." I'm in my office at the compound, not able to believe I sound more like a CEO than a fucking club president.

Shadow is pacing the room, while Savage drums his boot so hard against the floor, I can hardly hear myself think. I grunt at him and bark at Shadow to sit the fuck down.

"Look," Shadow says. "I got no problem moving

drugs, collecting debt, running games, but I agree with you. I got an old lady at home now. We need more ways to bring in clean money."

"Cash businesses." Savage shrugs. "We got a few, but we need capital to buy into them."

Shadow looks at me. "You thinking about your old lady? Salons? Nail tech? What?"

I shake my head. The last damn thing I need is to involve Poppy in anything that could be remotely less than legal. I'm not washing money through her shop or doing anything that can come back on her business.

We've got to get creative and tighter. I look to Savage. "I want all the prospects gone. Every one of 'em. Anyone who was friends with Dylan or came to us through him, gone."

Shadow doesn't look surprised. "Been waiting for you to say it."

"We'll need fresh blood," Savage says. "New recruits."

"No more kids," I say. "Not for a while. I want ex-military, guys with records. Anybody willing to work for what they want."

It goes without saying that they need to be loyal. I can't worry that some crackhead kid is going to decide to fuck my ex, steal from my clients, or just not fucking understand the code. We're brothers. Closer than family blood. We're blood by choice. I'd die for my kids, for Poppy, but if push came to shove, I'd also give my life for any of the men in this room. There was a time I thought I could say that about every man in this building. I know better now. And I don't like learning lessons the hard way.

"Put the word out," I say.

Shadow gets up and starts pacing again. "We run a couple more jobs for Elliott, a few more games through football season…"

I know what he's thinking. We can earn start-up capital in a matter of months. What would take a legit business years to create, we can get fully operational in a fraction of the time.

I nod. "Talk to Blade. Find out where we're flush and where we can scrounge cash fast." I put Shadow, my VP, on intel and Savage, our Sergeant at Arms, on recruitment. Between the two of them, I've got two out of three of my plans in motion. Now, all that's left is Viper.

I find him in the garage polishing a vintage Corvette.

I walk in and lean against a wall and don't say anything.

Viper keeps waxing the bumper, but he nods at me. "What do ya need, Prez?"

I walk over, considering how to phrase this. "Looking to expand."

"Business or membership?" he asks.

"Both," I confirm. "Looking to you for ideas."

Of all the guys, Viper is the only one I'd say would shoot first and ask questions later.

"Seems to me we need some housecleaning, with all due respect." Viper's polishing cloth slows as he says what could be a confrontational statement.

"That's why I'm fucking here," I tell him. "Prospects are gone. All of 'em. No more kids."

Viper nods.

"We need talent, maturity, and experience."

Viper nods again. "Where we looking for this talent?"

I say nothing. He knows. The only guys I'd trust are men my brothers trust.

"All right," he says. "About the work. How dirty we looking?"

He's asking a question I'm not sure I'm ready to answer. I've roughed up assholes who didn't pay their gambling debts. Shaken down cops for info. Paid off people to talk, paid off people to stay quiet.

"We need clean," I tell him. "To make the dirty a little less dark."

In the past, Viper's brought us what he called opportunities. Contract hits are nothing I'm interested in, but if we can expand and diversify, any short-term source of cash must be on the table.

We don't have cameras inside the garage, so I tell him explicitly what's a no-go for me. No trafficking. I don't abuse women, kids, or animals. No exceptions. No innocent victims.

We run through a list of possibilities. Some, I immediately shoot down. I'm not running guns. Too much federal scrutiny. I want to fly as far under the radar as I can. That means steady money, no flash. If the DEA or any other three-letter acronym gets a hard-on for it, I want to think a little further outside the box.

Viper's got the darkest past of anyone, except

maybe Savage, who's seen combat abroad. He doesn't talk about it ever, but he's stealthy, strong, and knows how to run an operation.

"You got your kids full time and an old lady," Viper says. But there's no judgment there. He's saying it because it's a fact. "You looking to take on more of a managerial role? Less boots on the ground?"

I chuckle. "Depends on the role and the ground you're talking about." It's important to me that my brothers know that, no matter how much changes—Shadow's married, I've got myself a live-in old lady and my daughters full time—I'm still, first and foremost, a member of the club.

Viper comes around the Vette and meets my eyes. "Change is the only constant," he jokes. "So, we change."

That we will. Especially if this club and all the people it loves and supports want to survive.

My phone buzzes with a call. I hold up my phone and leave the garage.

"Yo," I answer.

"You got a problem." Ed, as usual, minces no words. "The kid reneged on the plea. His attorney filed a motion with the court to withdraw the plea."

My blood boils, and I see nothing but red. "Not possible," I say, refusing to believe it. "He's been sentenced. This is a done deal."

"This isn't the playground, Phantom." Ed's sputtering mad. "This is a kid's life. He signed a sworn statement that he was coerced to enter the plea. Between you and me, I think the prosecutor wants to cut a deal and make him an informant. You taking him back if he gets out?"

I start to say fuck no, but then it occurs to me. There might be use for dear old Dylan after all.

"What're the odds the plea deal gets withdrawn? What happens then? He gets off scot-free?"

"Not likely," Ed says. "I don't know the ins and outs of criminal law. I only handle shit that crosses over into family law, but since you're involved in Dylan's case..."

"I know how we got here, Ed. But where the fuck does this go from here?" I demand, my hands shaking. I'm trying to control my temper. To see every possible angle.

"I don't fuckin' know, Phantom. He cuts a better deal and becomes an informant. Prosecutor drops the charges. Charges stick, and he rolls the dice and goes to trial. I don't have a crystal ball. I'm just calling to let you know what I do know."

I thank Ed and calm down. My mind's spinning. No matter what happens, I'm going to have both a problem and an opportunity on my hands. My entire life, I've been the guy who's turned shit sandwiches into steak dinners. This is going to be no different.

I call an emergency meeting and let my crew know what I do.

"Let me just take him out," Viper says. "He's a pissant problem with a simple solution." He holds his fingers like a gun, cocks them, then shoots.

"That's Plan D or even E," I say. "We've got to think smart about this."

"I say we do nothing," Shadow says. "Let the

system play its cards. We'll know what hand he's holding by the time the chips fall."

I nod. That's what I'm thinking.

My girls are safe.

Jax, Poppy, we're all safe.

"I'll have Ed keep us posted, but we're going to need someone on the inside and someone on retainer."

Savage nods. "I got the inside covered."

Blade shrugs. "We don't got anybody now, but I'll talk to Ed. See who he knows in criminal."

"I want an attorney who's clean," I tell them. "Somebody who defends the good guys."

"Those don't come cheap to guys like us," Blade says, rubbing his fingers together to represent big, big money.

I know. Nothing in life is easy, and I sure as hell know nothing is cheap.

"It's a turning point," I tell them. "We go big, or we go home."

No man in this room is a quitter. Every one of us has big dreams and a reason for being here. I have four reasons to go bigger than I ever have before. Working smarter, though, not harder.

I look at the club flag that's hanging up behind my desk.

History's about to be made for the club. Under my watch, we're going to be bigger, dirtier, better, and smarter than ever before. My family depends on it. My entire family. And that's all the motivation I need.

One month later

"Where are we going for dinner?" Poppy's talking as she sucks my cock, timing her words between each suck.

"Babe." I drive my fingers through her hair. "More cock, less talk."

She laughs and takes me so deep, I tremble down to my toes.

"Fuck," I hiss and throw my head back so hard I wouldn't be surprised if I gave myself a concussion. Pleasure shocks my system and nearly takes my breath away.

She hums around my shaft, flicking her tongue and pressing her thick lips along every ridge and vein. "Better?"

I grunt my approval and motion for her to turn over. "The only thing better is me seeing your ass."

She rolls onto her stomach and lifts her rear end in the air. The kids are in their rooms finishing their homework.

We're taking all the kids to dinner before Lori takes the girls to California for a weekend visit with their mom. She's taking Jax and a friend as well. They're going to hit Disneyland together to give Shayla and the girls a chance to experience something together that's safe and supervised so she doesn't compromise her sobriety. That means Poppy and I will have some time to ourselves.

Before everybody goes, we're sneaking in a few minutes of adult time.

I'm ready to put on a condom when my phone

rings. It's the alert I have for Savage when he's calling on the encrypted app. He wouldn't call if this weren't an emergency situation, so I groan but reach for the bedside table to grab the call.

"What?"

"He's getting out." Savage gets right to the point. "Dylan. I got a guy on the inside in processing. Your attorney won't get notified for another day, but looks like Dylan will be released tomorrow."

Fuck.

"We have options," Savage says. "But you need to make this call."

"What are they?" I climb out of bed and pace naked to the window. I hold up a finger to Poppy, who nods.

"Option one, he never makes it to processing," Savage says. "I can probably get that done, but we got to act fast."

"What else?" I bark. I don't like the idea of owing somebody on the inside anything. While I'd love to see Dylan meet his end on the filthy floor of a prison shower, I want to know what else we've got.

"Viper," Savage says. "We send Viper to meet him when he's released. He never makes it home."

So that's it, then. Our two plans are to have him taken care of inside or taken care of once he's free.

"You got anything else?" I ask.

"The usual," he tells me, and of course I know what that means.

"I'll make the call," I say. "Stand by your phone. I need five minutes."

I disconnect and head straight for the bathroom. I

drop the lid and sit on the can, rage and fear at war in my chest.

"Babe?" Poppy opens the door, which I didn't even bother to shut. She closes it behind her and grabs a bathrobe from a hook on the wall. She wraps herself up, then kneels on the cold tile beside me. "Phantom."

She puts a hand on my knee but doesn't say anything.

I want to tell her. I want to talk to her. To unburden myself of these shit choices. I want to provide for my family and keep shit in line. That's it. I want to beat up assholes who try to run out on their debts. I want to move shit to the people who want it and get paid for the risk. I do not want to start butchering my enemies. That's a one-way street, and I know the kinds of places that road will lead.

I sniff hard and look at Poppy. I can't say anything, but I search her face for answers. What's the right thing to do?

Poppy rests her cheek on my knee, planting a light kiss on my leg. We sit there quietly for a minute while I stew. The seconds are ticking by, and I need to make this call.

"There's always more than one solution to a problem." Poppy's voice is gentle. I'm assuming she heard enough of my conversation with Savage to know that I've been asked to make a call. She shifts her weight so her chin is on my knee and she can look me in the eyes. "If you think you only have two options, maybe you have three. If you think you only have three…" She shrugs. "You know what I've learned from you, Phantom?"

I look up to meet her chocolate-brown stare.

She continues, understanding that I'm in no state to talk this out. "Look at you and my mom, for example. She has every reason not to like you. To judge you. And yet, she adores you. Why? Because she knows that, no matter what you do, you have a code of ethics. You may not always do what she would do, what I would," she chuckles, "or what the laws in the state of Florida would tell you to do, but when you believe in something, you live and die by that code. I trust your code, Phantom. So should you."

She kisses my knee again before saying, "I'm going to go back to bed. We have a few more minutes if you want to finish what we started."

Then she gets up, leaves the bathroom, and shuts the door behind her.

I'm alone and naked, and yet I've never felt less alone. I think about Shayla and how easy it would have been to take care of her. It would be easy to take Dylan out. And God knows I like uncomplicated. But easy and uncomplicated are not the same thing.

There must be another way. A way to get Dylan out of our lives to buy us some time.

My mind whirls, and I think about Shayla and Dylan. Dylan and the fucking rats.

And then it comes to me.

I dial Savage back, and he answers on the first ring. "We're going with option three," I tell him. "I'll give you the details tonight. I gotta go fuck my old lady."

"I'll be waiting."

I end the call and leave my phone in the bathroom. I head back to bed and climb under the covers, taking Poppy in my arms.

"Thank you," I whisper, so quietly I don't think she can hear me.

But she does. I know she does.

She takes my soft cock in her hands and strokes it, rubbing me until I'm hard as a lead pipe. "Fuck me, babe," she whispers.

And I do.

EPILOGUE
POPPY

THREE MONTHS *later*

"So, you guys have no idea what you're getting? Or do you each know what you're getting, but you're just keeping it a surprise from each other?" Holly waits on a plush leather bench, furiously texting Tyler, I assume. She only texts her boyfriend that much, that fast, probably giving him a blow-by-blow of what we're doing.

"I know what they're getting." Jax looks up from his tablet and gives Phantom a grin.

Phantom puts a finger over his mouth.

Daisy crosses her arms over her chest. "No fair. How do you know when the rest of us don't?"

Jax shrugs a shoulder, and I stroke his hair. "Jax knows because he drew mine," I say.

Jax opens his mouth to say something, but Phantom shushes him again.

"Poppy? You can come on back." A girl with jet-black hair and teal-blue bangs—really well-colored, by the way—calls me back to her station. The tattoo shop has six chairs, each partitioned for privacy. Mine should only take about fifteen minutes, so I'm taking the kids for ice cream while Phantom gets his.

We decided to get tattoos to celebrate new beginnings. Shayla is back from rehab and will be taking the girls for scheduled visits, starting with spring break. The salon is doing great, and I have a fantastic tenant in my house. So fantastic, in fact, that she keeps telling her friends to come have their hair done by me. I must have six new clients on top of a great renter.

Phantom is celebrating because he did a really, really good thing. I know he's scared about it. Not that he's said, but because of what he doesn't say. I'm getting used to his silences, his grunts, and what he does decide to share. He decided after Dylan withdrew his plea deal, and the prosecutor dropped the charges, to send Dylan to rehab. Not the same one Shayla went to, but he sent Savage and Viper with Dylan on a plane to a reputable place in Michigan. The guys took Dylan, paid for everything, and told him he'd be welcome back in the club only after he finished rehab.

I know there's more to the story. Phantom likes to think I don't know that the guys think Dylan made a deal to be an informant or he's going to come back with a grudge. But I also believe that Phantom had a tough call to make. He stood true to his values, so despite the many answers I don't have about his business and what's going on with the club, I trust Phantom more now than ever.

So, we're getting celebratory tattoos. I decided to

add to the faded, messed-up heart that I got for Michael. Since Phantom loves tattoos, I designed something and asked Jax to draw it out. I have no idea what Phantom's getting, but he promised I'd get a kick out of the surprise.

Almost a half hour later, I have a brand-new tattoo on my ring finger. On the upper knuckle, I have a script P for Phantom. Added to the heart are delicate stars, one for each of the girls and one for Jax. The design is super thin and ladylike, and I even had Michael's heart touched up so it looks fresh and matches the rest of the design.

Now, instead of a faded heart that represents old memories, I have a story that combines my past, my present, and my future. Exactly the kind of tribute a great tattoo should be.

When I'm done, I take the kids for ice cream and wait for a text from Phantom. He was going to be a lot longer than I was, so I drove his truck and he rode his motorcycle to the tattoo parlor. After ice cream, I take the truck and drive the kids home, leaving Phantom for as long as his ink will take.

The kids are all tucked in when I hear the rumble of his bike pulling into the driveway. Even after all these months, I still get butterflies when I hear that sound. I think of his gorgeous eyes, his beard, his grunts, and I take off down the stairs to meet him.

"Hey," I say, banging into his chest. I pull him close for a hug, but he winces and lifts his arms. "Oh my God, I'm sorry. Where did you get it? Did I hurt you?"

He chuckles. "I'm fine. Come on, let's go inside."

We lock up the garage and head up to our bedroom. "The kids are going to want to see. Should I wake them?"

He shakes his head. "They'll see it tomorrow. I want you to be the first."

We go into our bedroom and shut the door. Phantom sits down on the bed and unbuttons his shirt. "So, remember when I had Jax come to the compound with me? When your mom met you and the girls for smoothies?"

I nod. "Of course."

"I asked Jax to start this for me then. We had to do a couple revisions based on the available space, but here's what I got."

He peels back the clear film and the white bandage that is keeping it dry. On his left pectoral muscle, right over his heart, he's added something to the tattoos he has for both Daisy and Holly.

"It's a poppy," I stammer, my eyes filling with tears. "Jax drew this?"

Phantom nods, and I lean closer. The design is still oozing a tiny bit of blood in spots, but I can make out a gorgeous, really detailed poppy flower. The center of the flower is shaped like a heart, and the stem and leaves curl around the Daisy and Holly tattoos, forming a larger heart.

"It's small," Phantom explains, "but I wanted Jax represented too." He points to three curling, vine-like things that come out stylistically from the stem of the flower. "If you look close, these three things are letters."

"J-A-X," I whisper.

I don't know what to say. I feel elated, giddy, emotional. I want to hug my son, our girls, Phantom. I can't contain the love that I feel. I truly have no words. I take a page from Phantom's playbook and say nothing. I just hold out my left hand.

"Fuck." He looks over the delicate designs. "Jax did this, too? God, babe. He's good. This is gorgeous."

He replaces the bandages and buttons up his shirt. "We'll have to be a little careful fucking," he laughs. "It's going to be tender for a few days."

I laugh with him because there's never been a truer statement. Phantom is a tender heart. A good man. My true love.

I climb onto the bed beside him and rest my head on his shoulder. "You know my tattoo was less expensive than Daisy's last hair color? Maybe we should send Jax to beauty school."

Phantom laughs. "He can do whatever he wants. With parents like us, he'll be okay."

"More than okay," I say, turning to kiss him. "If we have to be careful of your chest, I think that means I need to do most of the work," I tell him, sliding out of my sleep tee.

"I'm yours, babe. Use me any way you want."

I straddle his lap and kiss him, stroking his beautiful beard and tasting his perfect lips.

"Oh, I will, babe. I will. We have tattoos for each other now, so you know what that means."

Neither one of us says it because it doesn't need to be said.

Him. Me. Our family. Us.

Forever.

Want more sexy bossy bikers of Hurricane Heat MC?
Savage's Story is next!

>> Visit __menofinked.com/savage__
to learn more and get your copy.

♥ Men of Inked Reader Guide ♥

*Visit **menofinked.com/guide** to grab the extensive Chelle Bliss Reading Guide, which includes a family tree, printable guide, and information about the Gallo family saga.*

BECOME A MEMBER OF THE FAMILY...

Want a place to talk romance books, meet other bookworms, and all things Men of Inked? Join Chelle Bliss Books on Facebook to get sneak peeks, exclusive news, and special giveaways.

Want to be the first to hear about the next Men of Inked book or everything Chelle Bliss? Join my newsletter by visiting *menofinked.com/inked-news* or scan the QR code below.

ABOUT THE AUTHOR

I'm a full-time writer, time-waster extraordinaire, social media addict, coffee fiend, and ex-history teacher. *To learn more about my books, please visit menofinked.com.*

Want to stay up-to-date on the newest Men of Inked release and more? Tap here to join my newsletter or visit *menofinked.com/inked-news*

Join over 10,000 readers on Facebook in Chelle Bliss Books private reader group and talk books and all things reading. Tap here to become part of the family or visit at *facebook.com/groups/blisshangout*

Tap here to see the Gallo Family Tree or visit *menofinked.com/gallo-family-tree*

Where to Follow Me:

facebook.com / authorchellebliss1

instagram.com / authorchellebliss

bookbub.com / authors / chelle-bliss

goodreads.com / chellebliss

amazon.com / author / chellebliss

tiktok.com / @chelleblissauthor

pinterest.com / chellebliss10

LOVE SIGNED PAPERBACKS & SPECIAL EDITIONS?

Visit *chelleblissromance.com* for signed paperbacks and book merchandise.

UNTITLED